THE ROOF
IS ON *Fire*

HELL HOUSE 2

REALITY TV DRAMA

Dear Reader:

In Brenda Hampton's *Hell House*, she introduced us to six unique characters from some of her bestselling novels, placed them into a house and let the drama unfold.

It's reality television in book form, and readers will watch and guess which roommate is eliminated one by one. The author is a skilled storyteller who has entertained numerous fans with her tales, including more than twenty books. This is one hell house whose residents will surely bring pleasure with their survival tactics and cutthroat ways.

And stay tuned for the finale in the trilogy, *The Reunion Show*, where a winner will be declared. See if you can figure out who will be the strongest and last one standing in this clever concept.

If you haven't caught the first title in the series, an excerpt is included after the end of this novel.

As always, thanks for supporting the authors of Strebor Books. We always try to bring you groundbreaking, innovative stories that will entertain and enlighten. I can be located at www.facebook.com/AuthorZane or reached via email at Zane@eroticanoir.com.

Blessings,

Zane

Publisher
Strebor Books
www.simonandschuster.com

ALSO BY BRENDA HAMPTON
Hell House

ZANE PRESENTS

THE ROOF
IS ON *Fire*
HELL HOUSE 2

REALITY TV DRAMA
A NOVEL

BRENDA HAMPTON

SBI
STREBOR BOOKS
NEW YORK LONDON TORONTO SYDNEY

Strebor Books
P.O. Box 6505
Largo, MD 20792
http://www.streborbooks.com

ISBN 978-1-59309-538-3
ISBN 978-1-4767-4618-0 (ebook)
LCCN 2013950649

First Strebor Books trade paperback edition March 2014

Cover design: www.mariondesigns.com
Cover photograph: © Keith Saunders/Marion Designs

10...6...2 1

Manufactured in the United States of America

For information regarding special discounts for bulk purchases,
please contact Simon & Schuster Special Sales at 1-866-506-1949
or business@simonandschuster.com

The Simon & Schuster Speakers Bureau can bring authors to your live event.
For more information or to book an event, contact the Simon & Schuster Speakers
Bureau at 1-866-248-3049 or visit our website at www.simonspeakers.com.

The time was now. Somebody had to go. I suspected that it wouldn't be me. The last thing I recalled was when Roc gave me Tylenol and a glass of water. That was when we heard someone enter through the front door. To our surprise, it was Jeff. He spoke to us, then found the others and asked them to gather around. I wondered what was going on, because he looked to have something heavy on his mind. Maybe there was no fucking allowed in this house and Jaylin and Sylvia were about to get booted out. The rules mentioned nothing about intimacy, though, so I really wasn't sure why Jeff was here.

Either way, we all spread out on the couch to listen in. Jeff scratched his head and raked his fingers through his blond hair.

"The time has come for someone to be voted out of Hell House. There are six of you, and all six of you will decide who that person will be."

I shifted my eyes from one person to the next with much confusion on my face. All along, we thought that each person had to leave of their own free will, that no one could be voted out of here. This didn't make sense. I guess the same concern was on everybody's mind. We all spoke at once.

"What the fuck?" Roc said out loud. "You didn't say all of that from jump."

"I'm confused." Chase shrugged. "Why vote?"

"Trickery," Prince added. "This shit happens all the time."

Jeff raised his hands to get our attention. "Okay, everyone. Calm down. From the beginning, we made it clear that there may be some twists and turns in this competition. This is one of them."

I cocked my head back. "Well, I hope you don't decide to do a twist when it comes to uppin' the money. If you do, be prepared for me to twist your fuckin' neck. The one thing I don't play with is money."

"Jada, the money situation is good." Jeff cleared his throat. "But in order for you all to dwindle down to one, we must do it this way. So, take a minute to think about whom you all want voted out of here today."

"Today," Sylvia shouted. "Why today? It would be nice if you could give us a little more time to think about this."

"Unfortunately not. You must decide immediately, and one-by-one, I need each of you to go over to the computer and email me the name of the person you want to leave. At 5:00 PM, I will email you that person's profile and picture. Feel free to answer your fan mail before you leave, but after that, the person voted off must leave."

"This is terrible," I said. "I feel like I got to backstab somebody, and y'all already know I don't get down like that."

Jaylin stood and rubbed his hands together. "It's the rules, baby. Learn to follow them."

Without hesitating, he walked over to the computer. Logged in and typed in somebody's name.

"Done," he said, looking at Jeff.

My mouth dropped open. "Damn, it was that easy for you?"

He responded with a shrug. Afterward, Chase ran her trifling self over to the computer, logged in and did the same. She swiped her hands together and had the nerve to say, "Good riddance."

Then Sylvia almost broke her neck rushing to the computer to login. She typed in a name, then hit the backspace key to make a correction. "Oops, sorry," she said. She logged out and moved away from the computer.

"Y'all some cold muthafuckas." Roc sat at the desk in deep thought. He pondered for a minute, then slowly typed in a name. He also appeared happy about his choice.

Now, it was Prince's turn. I hadn't moved because these fools came off giddy about what they had to do. Prince laughed when he typed in a name, then said, "Done deal. Be gone, Biatch!"

What the hell! Really? Like it or not, it was my turn. I moved slowly over to the computer desk with my lips poked out. After I sat at the desk, I tapped my leg, thinking hard about who I wanted to go home. I didn't know whose name to type. I could think of at least one good reason why every person in this house should be sent packing. Some, I could think of several reasons. The decision didn't come easy for me, and I couldn't stop thinking about the money. Eventually, I forced myself to type in the name of the person I wanted to go home. I backed away feeling awkward, but hoping that the person leaving today wouldn't be me.

"Thank you, everyone," Jeff said. "Enjoy the rest of your day and say your goodbyes to everyone, just in case."

No one said a word. The room fell silent and all we heard was the front door shut.

"Well," Jaylin said, standing up and stretching. "It was fun while it lasted."

Roc smiled and cocked his neck from side to side. "Yes it was, but somebody must go. Too bad it won't be me."

Prince slapped his hand against Roc's. "I second that motion, my nigga. Won't be me either."

"What makes you all so sure?" Chase asked with a frown.

Roc's eyes shifted to Jaylin, and his eyes shifted to Prince. Neither of them said anything else, leaving some of us on pins and needles for most of the day.

When five o'clock rolled around, we all surrounded the computer desk, gazing at the twenty-seven-inch monitor. The room was so quiet that the only thing you could hear was hearts beating. My palms were sweating and my stomach tightened when the person's profile and picture came up on the screen. All eyes turned in the same direction. All I could say was, "Damn." She ain't have to go, but it was time for Sylvia to get the hell out of here!

Tears rushed to the rim of her eyes. She hurried to smack away a slow tear that rolled over her cheek. She swallowed hard and everyone waited for her to speak. Her eyes said it all; she was fuming. Her eyes were locked with Jaylin's, and neither of them broke their intense gaze. It was a nail-biting situation, so I took this as an opportunity to speak up.

"Ooooo," I said, looking at Jaylin with my hand on my hip. "After beatin' her pussy like that, did you vote for her to leave?"

His eyes shifted to me. The sly smirk on his face said it all. I had voted for Sylvia too, only because she was trifling. It was a tossup between her and Chase. I chose Sylvia because of her heated sex session in the closet with Jaylin. I didn't want her to have no more access to his goods and baby-making gravy.

While shaking my head, I pretended to be disgusted with Jaylin. "You did vote for her, didn't you? Talk about dir-tee. Pussy don't have no kind of value anymore. There was a time when a sista could get her mortgage paid for uppin' it. Now, the goodies ain't worth shit."

"Depends on whose pussy it is," Chase said with snap in her voice. "Some women don't have it like that, while others do. Unfortunately, Sylvia, you don't. So pack it up. You're going home."

Prince cocked his head back and sucked his teeth. "Soon, all of you peasants will be gone, so don't nobody get comfortable."

He walked away after Chase advised him to kiss her ass. She then cut her eyes at Sylvia. "Look. I voted for you as well, but don't take it personal. You played yourself. I did my best to try and warn you about going there with Jaylin. You never should have trusted him."

Sylvia put up her hand near Chase's face to silence her. "Chase, I don't want to hear your mouth right now. You know what you can do for me? You can get the heck away from me and go figure out something else to do with your time left here, other than chase after dick around this house."

"Don't be mad at me because playing by your own rules didn't work out. I'm not going to argue with you. Doing so will only prolong your stay, so goodbye."

Chase stormed away. Sylvia went into the kitchen, where Jaylin had moved to. I followed to be nosey.

"You voted for me?" she said with raised brows, directing her question to Jaylin.

When an irritated look washed across his face, I could tell this conversation was about to get painful for her. I tried to help by adding my two cents again.

"Duh, no. He voted for yo mama, not you. It's all the same, Sylvia, so why don't you stop embarrassin' yourself and go."

She swung around and lashed out at me. "Stay out of this, Jada! Mind your own business. Please!"

"Don't raise your voice at me, heifer. I know you're upset, but you'd better focus your anger on the man who broke yo back and now wants you out of the house! If anything, you need to stop searchin' for answers and do your best to leave here with some kind of diggity."

"It's dignity, you dumb, ghetto whore. I don't need help from somebody like you, so go somewhere and stuff yourself with cheesecake and hot apple pie. I got this. Trust me, I do."

I tightened my fists, but before I could crack that bitch upside her head, Roc grabbed my waist, pulling me away from her. All I could do was swing at the air.

"None of that, ma," he said, "Chill out."

"You need to let her go." Sylvia crossed her arms and pursed her lips. "She's a lot of mouth with very little action. All that crap you're doing doesn't scare me, and if you wanted to break away from Roc you could."

I loved the feel of Roc's strong arms secured around my waist. His touch made me relax a little. Besides, the *real* Sylvia was about to show up. The classy-lady act had flown out the window, and she was about to embarrass herself even more.

I twisted and turned to get away from Roc, but his grip was too tight for real. All I wanted to do was smack Sylvia for being so stupid, but he was preventing that from happening.

"You're real lucky," I hissed. "And only if I had a shoe."

Sylvia waved my threat off and looked at Roc. "I guess you voted for me too, huh?"

He didn't hesitate to answer. "Sorry, ma, but you made yourself an easy target. When I say don't take it personal, I mean that shit. See you at the reunion show. I hope you don't come strapped to that mutha."

Sylvia shrugged. "No need to. I guess you did what you felt you had to do."

Roc nodded and kept a tight hold on me as we made our way outside. I lifted my middle finger at Sylvia, positive that she knew what to do with it. She was now left to deal with Jaylin who had proven himself to be a plotting, cold motherfucker with no remorse.

Sylvia

It was no secret that I felt betrayed. In no way did I see this coming—not from Jaylin anyway. I still couldn't believe that he had voted for me to leave. I needed to hear it straight from his mouth if, indeed, that was the case. But after Jada and Roc left, Jaylin attempted to walk off. I reached out to grab his arm, giving it a light squeeze.

"Did you?" I questioned. "Yes or no."

He glanced at my grip on his arm, then peeled my fingers away from it.

"What difference does it make?" he said. "Jeff said no questions asked, you must go. I don't feel—"

"To hell with what Jeff said. I'm leaving, but I still want to know who you voted for. Why don't you man up and tell me?"

"Why don't you woman up and face reality. Your time here is up, Sylvia. Peace."

He walked smoothly toward the bedroom. To say I was shocked by the whole thing would be an understatement. I expected for the others, especially the women to vote for me, but I thought Jaylin and I had made a connection last night. A friendly connection where he would look out for me, as I had done him. How could I have been so wrong?

I charged after him as he went into the bedroom and sat shirt-less on the bed. His fineness was being ignored because his piercing gray eyes were filled with animosity toward me. Why? I hadn't a clue.

I sat on another bed in front of him so he could face me. "You say I should woman up and face reality, but what is the reality of this situation? Am I missing something?"

He got straight to the point and came off cold as ice. "The reality is you're going home. I suspect that you only have a few more minutes to get packed before someone will be here to get you."

I swallowed the baseball-sized lump in my throat, barely able to reply. "I'm okay with going home. If that's my reality, so be it. But my concern is with you. Why are you treating me as if last night never existed?"

"Don't concern yourself with last night. It was only sex between an eager man who needed to accomplish something and a horny-ass woman who got exactly what she wanted. Nothing more, nothing less."

My mouth was wide open. "Is that how you saw it? I found it to be much more than that. Horny or not, we made a connection. A connection that I, at least, thought would make me exempt from you casting a vote against me."

The gaze in Jaylin's eyes showed that he didn't care. He stroked his goatee, wet his lips, then elaborated more. "My vote was an easy one. I lost respect for you and wanted you to go. Boys will be boys, some friends will remain friends, but a woman who fucks them both doesn't get much respect in my book. A connection we did not have and I reject your fantasy. The only thing we had was satisfying sex, so stop fooling yourself. If you thought that pussy would sway my vote, sorry, you were sadly mistaken. Pussy that belonged to my friend doesn't move me like that, and the good and or bad of it don't supersede my brainpower. My brain makes decisions for me, not my dick that you managed to wet so well. You satisfied my appetite momentarily, but get real and recognize that all good things do come to an end."

I was speechless. Did he really just go there? A big part of me wanted to drop back on the bed and cry. But there was no doubt that I could handle his harsh words that shook me to the core. I had to keep a straight face so Jaylin wouldn't have the satisfaction of seeing me break down. For him to sit there and speak to me with so much coldness and cruelty, it said more about him than it did about me. The truth of the matter was…I was in a vulnerable state. I shouldn't have put myself in a situation like this one, and I regretted it. How stupid of me to think we'd made a connection.

Now that I had my answer, I got up from the bed and went to the closet to gather my things. I heard the bedroom door shut. I figured Jaylin had left the room. I closed my eyes, trying to fight back some of the hurt I felt inside. There was no doubt that I still had some work to do on myself. It started with getting my feelings under control, pertaining to Jonathan. It was because of him that I was here to begin with. It was because of him that I allowed Jaylin to go inside of me. I assumed that he would tell Jonathan everything that happened here, but at this point, so darn what. Girls will be girls, some friends will remain friends, and a real woman won't deny when she's had good dick inside of her. Jonathan would get an earful. I chuckled a bit from the thought, and after I packed, I sat at the computer desk to reply to the last piece of fan mail I'd gotten.

Hi, Sylvia. My name is Sasha Sutton and I'm from Montgomery, Alabama. When I read about you in Slick, I could relate to your experi-

ence with Jonathan. I, too, fell for my friend's boyfriend, but in the end, I wound up losing them both. They're now back together. I wondered how you would feel if Jonathan and Dana ever remarried. Also, do you feel as used as I do?

I adjusted the chair and placed my fingertips on the keyboard to respond to Sasha's questions.

I doubt that Jonathan and Dana would ever remarry. There was too much damage done. But if it somehow magically happened, I would be hurt. I get what you're saying about feeling used, and even though I don't want to seem like the victim here, I was put in a tricky situation. As my friend, Dana used me to lie for her. She often told Jonathan that she had been spending time with me, when in reality she was with her lover. She had no problem putting me in the middle of her lies, and I was put into a horrible situation where I had to lie to Jonathan when he asked about our whereabouts. Unfortunately, I wasn't a good liar as she was, and he was able to see right through me. I hated lying to him because I loved him. But he also made me feel used. It was my shoulder that he cried on when Dana had hurt him. It was my pussy that he dove into when he didn't have access to hers. I happened to be in the right place at the right time, but to this day, there is a part of me that still loves him. I'm aware that my lingering love really doesn't matter and some things in life can never be. Then again, I'm not one who can ever predict the future, so who knows? Maybe that wedding of his won't happen after all.

I heard a horn blow. When I rushed to the window, I saw a yellow taxi parked in front of the house. I figured it was waiting for me, so without any further ado, I thanked Sasha for her question, logged off the computer and grabbed my bags. With my head held high, I sauntered by everyone sitting in the living room and slammed the door to Hell House on my way out.

Chase

Simply put, women like Sylvia had to learn about men the hard way. I saw the setup coming a mile away. She seriously thought she had the upper hand when it came to men like Jaylin. I may have underestimated him too, but as soon as he came through the kitchen this morning and didn't say two words to Sylvia, I knew it was a wrap for her.

What I didn't expect was for Jeff to ask us to vote someone out of the house today. I didn't give it a single thought. Sylvia had to go. She was fake. With her going back and forth between Roc and Jaylin, that wasn't working for me. The next person I wanted to go was Jada. She was too much! I didn't care much for Prince either, but I preferred to be left in this house with three men and no other women.

My plan to get Jada out of here would be difficult, only because Jaylin and Roc seemed to like her. I wasn't so sure about Prince, though. I couldn't read him like the others, but I did peg him as being a no-good crook that would stab a best friend in the back. I wasn't sure how he felt about Jada, so I intended to pay more attention to him. Maybe he could help me get her out of here— who knows?

The breaking news about Sylvia leaving had everybody watching their backs and on edge. We all seemed distant, but when Jada recommended that everyone join her in the living room area for a late-night movie, we agreed. She popped popcorn and separated it into two round bowls. The movie we decided to watch was a horror movie. With a blanket covering me, I scooted over on the floor and sat next to Roc. Jada was only a few inches away from Jaylin on the couch and Prince was relaxing on a beanbag.

"Somebody needs to turn out the lights and start the movie," Prince said.

"You're the closest to the TV," Jaylin replied. "And besides that, I can't touch anything with all this hot butter on my hands. Without mentioning any names, somebody thought it was a bright idea to pour two sticks of melted butter over the popcorn."

Jada sighed and snatched the bowl from his hands. "Yo ass is always complainin' about somethin.' I would hate to be yo damn woman 'cause you ain't never satisfied. This popcorn is delicious. If you don't like it, you can always go get an apple."

Roc reached out to bump his knuckle against Jada's, approving of her buttered-down popcorn. "You did good, ma. I don't know what Jaylin gripin' about. This is exactly how I like my popcorn."

"You're you and I'm me," Jaylin countered while holding out his hands. "This shit is too buttery and greasy. Look at my hands. I can jack myself off with hands like these."

"I'd be happy to watch," I said with a wide smile on my face.

Jaylin ignored my comment, but Jada didn't. "Didn't you learn anything from what happened to Sylvia? She came up in here sanctified and prayin' over meals, but left out of here a scorned ho. Stop bein' so desperate. If a man don't want you, he just don't want you. It's apparent that Jaylin ain't interested."

"Shhh," Prince said, dimming the lights. "I'm gettin' ready to start the movie, so y'all need to be quiet."

I paid Prince and Jada no mind. No words could describe how I felt about her. I turned around to question Jaylin.

"Am I coming off as being desperate to you? And if you're not interested, wouldn't it be wise for you to say so? That way, people aren't likely to assume anything, as Jada clearly has."

"Look, keep me out of it," Jaylin said. "I'm trying to watch the movie, but not before I go wash my hands."

He got up and stepped over Jada on his way to the kitchen to wash his hands. She frowned at first, but then smiled as her eyes followed the cargo shorts that hung at his waist.

"Daang." Jada licked her lips. "What's up with all that junk in yo front? Why don't you go put on a long shirt to cover all of that up, 'cause you may mess around and get raped up in here."

"Looking forward to it," Jaylin said while washing his hands.

I couldn't help but to laugh. It was a good thing that I wasn't the only one who noticed the mountain-sized bulge in his shorts. I wondered if he was hard. If so, who or what was possibly on his mind? Not to give it too much attention, when Jaylin returned to the couch, I scooted even closer to Roc. He seemed annoyed and looked straight ahead at the TV. I guess I had some making up to do, so as the movie got started, I crossed my leg over his and held on tight to his bicep.

"Have you seen this movie before?" I whispered to him.

"Nah. I don't do movies that often."

"Neither do I. But this should be fun."

Fun was an understatement. Midway through the movie, Roc and I had tuned it out. We took shots of Patrón, and I kept rubbing and touching on his goods underneath the blanket. He continued to move my hand away from his package, but he finally gave in and let me have my way. I was doing my best to make him bust a nut, but he wouldn't do it. His fire-red eyes fluttered, he squirmed around, and he kept on clearing his throat. A deep breath escaped from his mouth, helping to keep him calm. I was amazed by his control. Maybe I needed something more than butter from the popcorn on my hands to stroke him, but I was trying to keep our playtime as undercover as possible.

"Here." I passed the remaining popcorn in the bowl back to Jada so she could eat it. If she knew where my hands had been, she would've slapped me. Obviously, she didn't care and gobbled down the popcorn so quickly that she was about to choke.

"Mmmm," she said, smacking her lips and licking her fingers. "Y'all popcorn taste awfully salty. It could use a little more butter, though."

She hopped up from her seat, but Jaylin removed the bowl from her hand. "Sit down and watch the movie. You don't need any more popcorn, and all this moving around and talking is a damn distraction."

"Hold up, Curly Top. My daddy died when I was three years old. I would appreciate if you wouldn't go there like that with me, and no man is goin' to tell me what I shouldn't be eatin'. And for the record, yo ass the one distractin' me by tryin' to have control."

Prince turned around with a twisted face. "Shhh. Shut the hell up so I can hear the damn movie."

Jada snatched the bowl of popcorn from Jaylin's hand and stormed off. She was such a brat. Jaylin asked her nicely to come back. From the smirk on his face, he appeared to get a kick out of her foolishness. Prince, however, went off.

"She's a silly-ass bitch, I swear. I'll be so glad when she get out of here."

It was good to know that we were on the same page. I made a mental note to hook up with him about making sure that happened.

For now, I got back to Roc, who had my hand full with his hard meat. I couldn't wait to find out what his pipe felt like inside of me. I whispered near his ear, sharing how wet I was.

"Umph. That wet, huh?" he said.

"I would rather show you than tell you. Why won't you let me?"

"In due time, I will. Just sit on that for a while and think about how good it's going to feel when you get a chance to take it all in."

I smiled with seduction in my hazel eyes. "I've been thinking about it since day one. This waiting game is depressing. I'm not quite sure what it is that we're waiting for. I said it once and I'll say it again—if you won't tell, neither will I."

"That's good to know, because the one person I can't stand is a snitch."

"Well, my lips are sealed…until you have something better to put between them."

Roc nodded, then filled our shot glasses with more Patrón. "Here's to me bustin' a nut when the time permits it to happen."

"I'll definitely drink to that."

We clinked our glasses together, then shot the alcohol to the back of our throats. By now, Jada had returned to the couch and was resting her head on Jaylin's shoulder. She pretended to be so frightened by the movie and was damn near sitting on his lap.

"I can't look!" she shouted and covered her face with a pillow. "Is he goin' to kill her or not?"

Prince was irritated by her ongoing nonsense. "If you would silence the noise by closin' your big-ass mouth, you'll see what's gon' happen."

"Do you have a problem with me, little boy?"

"Yes, I do. But now ain't the time for me to go there with you 'cause I'm tryin' to see what's up with this movie."

"That makes two of us. So do me a favor and don't say anything else to me."

Prince mumbled something like "stupid bitch" underneath his breath and that about did it for the movie. Him and Jada started going at it. I was so surprised when Jaylin took up for her.

"Listen, man. All I'm saying is cool out with the 'bitch' thing. That ain't no way to refer to a woman, and you've been going there since we've been here. Your words are starting to rub me the wrong way. They're insulting."

Prince stood and shrugged. "I don't give a fuck. Tell that bitch to keep her distance from me, or else I can promise the both of y'all that blood will shed. I ain't ever had respect for no chick with that much mouth. Where I come from, you can get knocked on yo ass for makin' that much noise."

"And where I come from, stupid fools are capable of dyin' from the hands of an angry black woman. Keep on talkin' yo mess and threatenin' me, Prince. I'mma introduce you to how I play Show, Not Tell."

Roc and I had heard enough. We were pretty messed up from drinking Patrón, so we went outside to chill on a lounging chair. I could still hear Jada and Prince arguing, so I eased on top of Roc, straddling him. As he dropped the chair back, I brushed my fingertips down his carved chest and traced my fingers along his numerous tattoos. I then lifted his wifebeater to suck and bite at his nipples.

"Why…why are you goin' to make me do this with you?" Drunkenness was trapped in his narrowed eyes and his voice slurred. "Why can't you just let a nigga be good and stay on the right track?"

I backed away from his nipple and sat up straight. The strap to my silk pajama top had fallen off my shoulder, exposing my firm, left breast. Roc gazed at it without a blink.

"Damn, ma, you got me wide open right now. Did you put a li'l somethin'-somethin' in my drink?"

"No," I said with a smile. "And only if you were willing to have me wide open. You want me to let you be, but unfortunately, I can't. I want you, Roc. Want you more than I have ever wanted any man in my life."

That wasn't the truth, but I felt like saying it. I could see him getting weak for me.

"Is that right? If I didn't know any better, I'd say you'd be sayin' the same shit to Jaylin if he was out here with you, instead of me. With that in mind, I need to pull back on this. Maybe it will happen, just not tonight."

Roc placed my strap back on my shoulder, covering my breast. He sat up and I had to remove myself from his lap. Before going back into the house, he kissed my cheek and squeezed my ass at the sliding door. I said not one word. Deep inside, I knew that tonight wasn't looking good for me, but the days ahead were promising.

Prince

Another week inside of Hell House had passed us by. The cooking and cleaning schedules were all jacked up. Many of us hadn't been following the rules. I'd been keeping my distance from Jada, but the dirty looks she kept giving me had me swoll.

As I left the bathroom the other day, Chase caught up with me. She wanted to know if we could work on a plan to get rid of Jada. My suggestion was that we do whatever it took to make it happen and I was down with Chase's ideas.

I was also down with Chase leaving, but that little task was left up to that nigga Roc. He'd been slipping. To be frank, all Jaylin, Roc and me had to do was vote her ass out of here. Then it would be a done deal.

"Who says that Jeff will let us vote like that again?" Roc said as we sat outside eating breakfast. "I doubt that he gon' make it that easy for us."

"We really don't know what that white boy will do, but if we have to vote again, are you down with votin' Chase out of this mutha or not?"

"Fool, what do you think? Why would you even think that I wouldn't be?"

Jaylin spoke up before I did. "Because you've been on her these past few days like flies on shit. Wherever she goes, you go. You ain't caught up, are you?"

"Is that what you niggas think? Y'all think I'm slippin' over some twat? Let me clear this shit up right here and now. I intend to be the last man standin'. When all is said and done, I will be. I have plans for Chase; plans that require me not to utilize my dick to get her to vacate the premises. I know that was your strategy, Jaylin, but I'm travelin' a different route because I got a lot to lose goin' there. Chase ain't worth me fuckin' up my shit at home. So I'mma keep playin' my cards how I wish to, whether you niggas like it or not."

Jaylin hurried to speak again. "I don't give a damn how you play your cards. All I'm saying is the clock is ticking. I did my part, now it's time for you and Prince to step up and do y'alls. If not, the game will change, and when we start playing solely by my rules, everyone will lose. Including you, Roc. You won't be the last man standing—I can promise you that."

He guzzled down his orange juice, awaiting a response from me or Roc. I sensed an argument brewing, so I stood to go inside.

"Sit down," Roc said, sucking his teeth. "I need to say this to both of y'all."

I hesitated, but sat back down at the table.

"I got Chase, Prince got Jada, and, Jaylin, you can do whatever the fuck you want to. When the three of us are the last ones in this house, I'mma need you niggas to be ready for what's gon' swing y'all way. It will get ugly, but that's because I really don't like either one of you muthafuckas. But my word is bond, and Chase will be out of here by the end of this week."

This time, Roc stood to walk away. Jaylin shouted loud enough for him to hear. "The feeling is mutual. But I have a feeling that when all is said and done, Chase leaving here will be left up to me.

You're too weak, Roc. This game may be too hard for a man who keeps choking up about the love he has at home. You may want to scrap this and hurry back to all that love you insist you're missing out on. By all means, I'm sure it's waiting for you."

Jaylin had Roc's attention. He came back over to the table and folded his arms in front of him, displaying a devious smirk. "Weak? Nah, ain't nothin' about me applies to that definition, but I can show you better than I can tell you. As I continue to do me, I'mma need for you to sit back, chill, clip yo loud mouth shut and learn somethin'. That goes for you too, Prince. If y'all know what's good for you, y'all will stop slippin' at the mouths about me and Desa Rae. Meanwhile, suckers, I have a job to do. One that will pay off for me, as it always does."

I didn't say shit and neither did Jaylin. Both of those fools had too much mouth for me. Talk like that always got brothas caught up. The less said, the better. I already knew who the victorious one would be, so there was no need for me to run around here boasting about it. Instead, I went inside with Jaylin and listened to him complain about how nasty the house was. He'd been sending Jeff emails almost every day, begging and pleading for him to send a maid service to come clean up.

"I don't see how people live like this," Jaylin fussed, then tossed one of Jada's pink house shoes in the trashcan. The shoe was in the middle of the kitchen floor. I didn't understand why he was so hot—to me, the house was clean. Yeah, we had a few items here and there, but it was nothing to get swoll about.

He rushed over to the computer to see if Jeff had responded to his emails about the maid service. Jeff had responded and attached several links in the email for Jaylin to reach out to the maid service of his choice.

"It's about damn time," Jaylin said, clicking on the links and go-

ing to each of the web sites. This fool was anal and he took cleaning too serious. I didn't have time to entertain his issues. Instead,
I went into the bedroom to change clothes so I could lift some
weights.

Dressed in jean shorts and an oversized Bob Marley T-shirt, I
made a move to the workout room. But as soon as I got to the
kitchen, I saw Jada standing in a red sweat suit with the refrigerator open. She looked like Santa Claus, without the beard. I ignored
her and started whistling. She closed the refrigerator and called
my name.

"What?" I replied.

"I found my house shoe in the trashcan. Did you throw it away?"

"No, I didn't. But what if I did?"

Her neck started to roll. "If you did, then we got ourselves a big
problem. Did you or didn't you?"

The sassiness of her voice, and tone reminded me too much of
the women in my past, especially my mama's. I didn't like to be
talked to any kind of way and Jada was about to find herself in
unfamiliar territory.

"I don't give a damn about your raggedy pink house shoe. That's
what you get for leavin' it in the middle of the floor. Stop bein' so
fuckin' lazy. Then you won't find yourself with those kinds of
problems."

As I moved toward the sliding door to exit, Jada charged after
me. She grabbed the back of my shirt, pulling it so tight that it
nearly choked me. Double my size, she slung me around, almost
causing me to skid on the floor. I caught my balance, though, and
transformed myself into the madman I hadn't been in a long, long
time. Anger crept up on me like a thief in the night. This time, I
wasn't tripping like I was when Jaylin had fucked me up. I was

fully alert to what was going on, and when she pushed my face with her hand, I tore into my bottom lip, preparing myself to go after her like I was battling in the streets. Before I knew it, I tightened my fist and hit her with an uppercut to the chin. It was enough to stand her up straight, but not to silence her.

"Motherfucker." she shouted while holding her chin. Before she said anything else, my face twisted beyond recognition. I landed a straight punch directly to her right eye. Her head jerked back, and as I saw her eyes roll to white, that was when she fell back. She hit the floor—hard. But in no way was I done with her yet.

"You want some of me!" I yelled while punting her midsection like a football. "What you got to say now, bitch! If you want to act like a nigga, I'mma treat you like one!"

As Jada shielded her head with her arms, I tried to stomp the life out of her.

"Stoooop!" she howled. "Somebody help me, please! This nigga crazy!"

"Well, now you know, don't you?"

Since I couldn't get at her face like I wanted to, I pounded the back of her head with my fist. I wanted to knock her unconscious, but it wasn't long before Roc rushed into the kitchen to save her from an ass-kicking that wasn't going to end anytime soon.

With hella force, he slammed his body into mine like a head-on collision. He then lifted me at my waist, carrying me backward to the refrigerator, then crashing me into it. My back cracked, leaving me with a burning sensation flowing up and down my spine.

"Have you lost yo muthafuckin' mind?" he shouted as he held me against the refrigerator. "Fool, what's wrong with you?"

"Nigga, that bitch put her hands on me! Let me the fuck go or else it's gon' be you and me."

"It's already you and me. Chill the fuck out and calm yo ass down!"

Wanting Roc out of my space, I pushed him back with force; force that caused him to stumble backward and then go after me again. This time, he grabbed my shirt and ripped it. He drew blood when he cracked his head against mine, head-butting me. I instantly got dizzy, especially when his head bumped into my mouth, splitting my lip. I guess I now knew why they called him Roc—his blows felt like stones. I could barely stay on my feet, but when I looked over his shoulder and saw Jada charging at me with a knife in her hand, I broke away from his grip and took off. The shiny blade had my name written all over it.

Jada shouted as she chased me around with the knife held up high. "You gon' die today! I swear to God that you will see Him soon."

I was fucked up, no doubt, but so was Jada. Blood stained the front of her sweat suit, her lip was swollen and busted, and her bruised eye was damn near shut. Still, she was only a few feet away from me when Jaylin called for her to put the knife down.

"Give it here," he calmly said, standing between us with a white towel wrapped around his waist. Obviously, he didn't hear what was going on because he was in the shower. "He ain't worth it, baby. Let it go and allow this fool to get out of here."

Tears were streaming down Jada's face as she continued to hold the knife in her trembling hand. Her demon-like eyes were locked with mine. It was no secret that the bitch really wanted to kill me.

"Move, Jaylin," she said while sobbing and barely able to catch her breath. "I...I want him dead!"

"No you don't. Calm down and think about what you're doing. Think, Jada, before you do something that you'll regret."

She calmed down—a little. That was when Jaylin held her in his arms. "I swear I want to kill him," she cried with her face buried in his chest. "I can't let him leave here without killin' him."

Good luck with that. And little did she know the feeling was mutual. I damn sure wasn't about to go down like this, but with Roc and Jaylin turning their backs on me, it was apparent that my time here was up. That was made clearer to me when Jeff and one bodyguard entered the house to escort me out.

"Gather your things, Prince, and go. What you did was totally uncalled for," Jeff said.

I got defensive. "What did I do? I guess you didn't see what she did. She put her fuckin' hands on me first. None of this would've gone down like this, if she hadn't touched me. If I gotta go, her ass needs to go, too!"

Jada broke away from Jaylin's embrace and rushed off to the bedroom. She slammed the door behind her. Jeff went after her, but he said the door was locked and he couldn't get in.

"Jada, unlock the door," he pleaded. "Do you need a doctor? If so, we want to get you one."

A doctor? What about me? All these suckers were catering to the Drama Queen and she was the one who kicked the whole thing off. Jaylin and Roc stood near the bedroom door shooting crazy looks in my direction. They also asked Jada to open the door. Chase stood with her arms folded and lips poked out. We could all hear shit being tossed around inside of the bedroom and a whole lot of grunting and foul-mouth talking was going on. I suspected Jada was throwing a tantrum. It wasn't until the body-guard kicked the door open when we saw what she had done. She had cut up some of my clothes, and shredded pieces were strewn around the room. She sat on my bed, slicing my Air Jordans in half, as if she was carving a turkey.

"Grrrrr," she growled with gritted teeth and flung my shoe at me when I was in her sight.

"Let me ask this again," I said. "I'm the one who has to go, right? Not her."

Jada raised her voice and threatened me. "Whether I stay here or not, you'd better go now or leave here as a corpse. I'm not playin' when I say your life is on the line for doin' this shit to me."

I waved her off. "Yeah, yeah, yeah, whatever. I don't give a fuck about leavin' here, but yo ass needs to start packin', too."

"I don't think it's fair to Prince if Jada is not asked to leave," Chase said. "This kind of behavior should not be tolerated. I don't feel safe with how she's utilizing that knife."

Jada frowned and gave Chase one of the dirtiest looks I'd seen from her thus far. I was glad that Chase had come to my defense. She was right. Jada needed to go.

Jeff turned to Roc and Jaylin. "What are you guys' takes on this? Should Jada go or stay? Are the two of you uncomfortable with her staying here? Is it fair that Prince is the only one we're asking to leave?"

Jaylin looked at Roc, and then he looked at me. "I've been in situations where I came close to gettin' down like that too, but you got some serious issues, bro. On a for real tip, you need to get up out of here and deal with those demons pullin' at you. As for Jada, she stays."

"I second that," Jaylin said. "No statement will come from me, other than Prince needs to go."

Jaylin walked off and went back into the bathroom. Roc went further into the bedroom and took the knife from Jada. Chase rolled her eyes, saying that it was a damn shame that I was asked to leave. I thought so too, but nobody saw things my way.

Jeff took Jada outside to cool off while I packed my things to leave. Once I was finished, I plopped down in front of the computer and took care of the last piece of fan mail I'd gotten. I scratched my head as I read a message from James from New Jersey.

What's up, Prince? My question for you is simple. Why blame other people for your fuck-ups and not take responsibility for your life? The answers to your troubles revolved around violence, but why not use your head to get out of the unfortunate situations you found yourself in? My advice would be for you to seek prayer. Brotha, you truly need it.

All I could do was shake my head. Everybody had the answers to correcting my problems. I bet any amount of money that James' life was more fucked-up than mine, yet he was trying to offer me advice. I almost broke my fingers trying to get my point across to this fool.

My house nigga with no trigger from New Jersey, what in the fuck are you talking about? The fact is, my Mama made some bad-ass choices that affected her life and mine too. Period. She is to blame for a lot that has gone on in my life, but as a lifelong Street Soldier, I took responsibility for things that affected me and handled my situations as best as I could. Feel free to talk yo shit all you want to. Feel free to shake yo head and point yo finger while you're at it, but I'll say this and leave it there. A man like you couldn't make it one day in my world. You don't understand it, and niggas like me are built to last. The question is, are you? Hell no, so therefore, I'mma need you to pray for yourself. Peace, bruh, holler back, but save all the bullshit I'm not trying to hear for another time.

After I finished with my response, I stood and cocked my hat on backwards. Jeff and his bodyguard escorted me out the front door.

"This is messed up," I complained to Jeff as he went to his car. "At least, can a nigga get a ride back to the hood?"

"A taxi is on the way. I'll stay with you until it gets here. But if you don't mind, I must say this to you before you go. You must learn how to control your anger. I'm not saying that Jada didn't start that fight, I watched everything unfold. You, however, should not have gone after her like you did. She's a woman, Prince. For God's sake, she's a beautiful woman who didn't deserve what you did to her. You should've just walked away."

His words pissed me off so bad that I started to go after him. Maybe I did have some anger issues that needed to be worked out, but they wouldn't be dealt with today.

"First of all, Jada ain't no woman. Just because she has a pussy, that does not make her one. She's a fuckin' bully that needed to be put in her place. You couldn't possibly expect for me to stand there and let her choke the shit out of me and not do anything. You, along with everybody else, made the call for me to leave here, so I'm done. I have no regrets. If that bitch ever put her hands on me again, she will get a repeat of what went down today."

Thankfully, Jeff didn't get a chance to respond because the taxi pulled up to get me. I got in the backseat, stung by what had happened, yet grateful that I would never have to see any of these motherfuckers again. Or, at least, not until the reunion show that I was now looking forward to.

Jaylin

It had been a long day. Too long, but I wasn't ready to call it a night. I had too much on my mind. After what had happened between Jada and Prince, it made me think about the times I was provoked to choke the shit out of Nokea for dating Collins and for her giving the pussy to another man. I also thought about when I fucked up Scorpio for lying to me about being a stripper and for having sex with my cousin, Stephon. There was no doubt that a man could be pushed, but Prince had gone too far. Jada was messed up. No matter what she had done to him, she didn't deserve to be treated like that.

I didn't want to take sides, but I had to. Prince was too much trouble, but there was something inside of me that felt for the brother. My hope was that he got his shit together.

Instead of getting in bed, I sat outside on a lounging chair, listening to jazz on my headphones and drinking Remy, no ice. I was on my third glass when I saw Chase and Jada come outside with their sleepwear on. They were full of giggles and seemed chummy, considering the attitudes they had with each other earlier. I removed the headphones so I could hear what Chase had said.

"Come again," I said.

"I promise you I will come for you anytime, Jaylin. But what I said was, I see you have the right idea, pertaining to the drink in your hand."

She smiled and sat next to me with a drink in her hand. Jada sat on the edge of my chair, drinking a wine cooler.

"We couldn't get any sleep with Roc snoring so loud," Chase said. "He's in there sweating, moaning, and talking in his sleep. When we tried to wake him, he went off on us."

"Sooo, we came out here to see what you were up to. We ain't interrupin' nothin', are we?"

I shrugged. "Just my thoughts, but maybe that's a good thing." I looked at Jada's eye that was nearly shut. By morning, I was sure her face would be even more swollen and her eye would be completely shut. "Did you put some more ice on that?"

"Yeah, I did, but my face kept feelin' numb. I'll be okay, Daddy, so stop worrin' about me."

"You may be okay on the outside, but scars like that can affect you for a lifetime. You know that, don't you?"

Jada looked down while biting her nail. "I know. But Prince ain't the first man that I had to get down and dirty like that with. I used to mess with this dude, Kiley, and we used to go toe-to-toe like that. He ain't never do me like Prince did, but we had plenty of fights that left me banged up."

Chase spoke up as well. "Sounds like a relationship I was involved in, too. But I had no problem defending myself. I came so close to cutting his dick off, and when I burned down his house, he knew I wasn't playing."

"Damn." I looked at Chase with my eyes wide. "Remind me not to fuck with you, especially if you're cutting off dicks and burning down houses."

Chase laughed. "I wouldn't do that to you, but y'all men need to stop playing. A lot of women put their hearts into relationships, and men need to be held accountable for breaking our hearts."

While listening to their situations, I gave them the best advice I could. "Look, this relationship shit is simple. Stop jumping into relationships with your hearts all into it. Y'all give too damn much sometimes and you got to hold yourself accountable for how much you choose to give."

"You don't have to tell me twice," Chase said. "I learned that the hard way. No man will ever have my heart again, but the ones I am attracted to are welcome to my, well, you know…my good pussy."

Jada high-fived Chase and they laughed.

"I know that's right," Jada said. "I'm a bit more selective with givin' up the goodies, but Jay Bay-bee you can get it! All of it. Just tell me when, where, how, and what position I need to form myself into, and I will do it."

I blushed and continued to drink Remy as they teased me with the truth.

"You damn right he can get it," Chase agreed. "But, unfortunately, he acts like he doesn't want it. What can I, and or Jada, do to make you want *it?*"

I sat my empty glass on the table and cleared my burning throat. "There's no secret, but I'd like to think that I'm selective when it comes to sex."

Jada pursed her lips. "Meanin', you only select women with hour-glass figures, long hair, light-bright or white skin, and with big-ole asses. Full-figured, brown-skinned women like me don't stand a chance, do we?"

"My taste is totally the opposite of what you just said. There are certain things that I prefer a woman to have, but I'm not going to get into all of that right now."

"Fine," Chase said. "But you still haven't answered my question. What does it take, Jaylin, to shake things up with you? Sylvia may be gone, but I'd like to think that she fell short at providing what you really needed."

"Shiiiit." Jada slapped her leg and laughed. "It didn't sound like nothin' fell short to me. His ass was whimperin' while in that closet too, so somethin' with her must've been on point. I suspect that Sylvia's head game was up to par. Was it or was it not?"

Yeah, it was, but I wasn't going to admit it. "Listen, let's end this conversation about Sylvia, and about who or what I prefer. It's not getting us anywhere. Besides, I'm getting kind of tired. Ready to call it a night."

"Awww, damn," Jada whined, then pouted. "Don't go yet, Jaylin. I'll change the subject, right after you tell me why you ain't married, how many women you got, and if or when I can have one of your babies?"

Chase added her two cents. "Good questions, Jada, but I want to know if you ever had a threesome before. Can Jada and I perform oral sex on you at the same time, and wouldn't you like to see us in very compromising positions?"

Jada's jaw dropped, but I smiled at the thought. "Wha— Wait a minute, bitch. I, Jada Mahoney-Jacobs-Schmidt-Abrams, don't get down like that. I've been married three times, to men, and I'm strictly dickly. I can handle Jaylin all by myself and an extra mouth will not be needed."

I had to clear things up for Jada. "Two mouths are always better than one, trust me on that tad bit of information. But I'm not married anymore because I don't want to be. I don't keep count of the women I date, and I'm always open to having more babies. Threesomes are welcomed, oral sex is a plus. and I'd be delighted to see any sexy woman in a position of my choice."

"You ain't said nothin' but a word," Jada slurred. She appeared woozy as she stood up and guzzled down the remaining liquid contents in the bottle. She slammed it on the table. "Somebody, give me some slow, come-fuck-me music so I can show dis' handsome man what I'm workin' wit'."

Chase giggled and cheered Jada on. "Show'im, girl. Give'im those babies he want and work yo position."

I sat back in the chair, watching as Jada climbed on the wrought iron table in her hot pink, short, silk robe. Underneath was a tight white T-shirt, and she had on yellow panties with smiley faces on them. As I could see clearly underneath her robe, her massive ass swallowed the panties that were way too little. And the more and more she dipped down to no music, her crack ate them up. I told her to get down, but she ignored me.

"Heeeey," she sang while snapping her fingers. She removed the rubber band from her sandy brown hair and teased it wildly with her fingers. After that, she put two fingers in her mouth, sucking them. "Tell me, baby. Do you want meeee? 'Cause I want choooo."

Almost falling, her drunk ass held on to the umbrella pole that was already leaning. I predicted that this was going to get real ugly. All I did was cover my face in disbelief, unable to look at her. Chase moved my hands away from my face, encouraging me to watch.

"She putting on her best Prince impersonation for you, and you won't even watch. Come on, Jaylin. Be a good sport."

Jada started doing the tootsie roll, then she popped, locked and dropped it—her robe. She took it off, tossing it to me.

"Go Jada, go Jada," Chase chanted. "Go, but don't hurt yourself, girl."

Jada was sucking it up. Her lips were tooted in the air, her panties had disappeared in her crack, and booty dimples were on display.

I had definitely seen enough. I stood to help her down from the table.

"Baby, come on. That's enough. That was good, and now it's time to go to bed."

She squatted to my level and rubbed her index finger along the side of my face. "Did I hear you mention a bed? Or are you goin' to reject me because you can smell hot, greasy fish?"

I could've died laughing, but I held back. Playful seduction was trapped in her eyes as she batted her lashes.

Before I could answer her question, the motherfucking table tilted slowly to the side, causing me to move out of the way so it wouldn't crash down on my feet. Jada, however, hit the pavement. She rolled from side to side on the ground, complaining of a broken back.

"Oh my Jesus!" she shouted. "I…I think I broke somethin'!"

Chase was unable to help because she was hollering from laughter. I kept shaking my head, but had to make sure Jada was okay.

I reached out my hand to help her off the ground. "See, that's what you get for playing."

She smacked my hand away. "I'm not playin'! I can't move, so you gon' have to pick me up and carry me."

"Like hell, baby. I told you not to get up there. You knew that table wasn't sturdy enough to hold you."

Jada quickly sat up, seeming to be okay. "If it was Roc, he would pick me up. This the last time I put myself out there for you. You didn't even catch me, and shame on you for allowin' me to fall and scar up my ass. My head feel busted too."

"Your head looks fine to me. Since you're so hurt, let me go inside and get Roc to come out here and help you."

"You do that," she said as I walked away to go inside. "Jaylin!" she shouted.

I turned. While still on the ground, she opened her legs wide and flashed her goodies. "I forgive you for bein' so uncarin', but you know you want this, don't you? I can see it in your heavenly eyes."

"My eyes are known for implying things that I don't mean, but if you shave that hairy bush we may have ourselves a deal. Until then, I want no part of the pussy."

"Screw you! That's why yo dick crooked. Nah!"

When I got inside, I had to snicker at Jada's silliness. Chase was only a few feet behind me. She reached for my arm before I went into the bedroom.

"Hey you," she said. "We had a good time tonight, didn't we?"

"No doubt."

"And, uh, forgive me for being so blunt, but I'm the kind of woman who speaks my mind. I meant what I said about shaking things up with you. I don't know which one of us will have to leave here first, but I hope that I get a chance to leave here with the same experience as Sylvia. Is that possible?"

"Could be, but I'm not one to predict tomorrow. My concern is your desire to shake things up with Roc as well. And since I'm the kind of man who speaks my mind, I'll say this. I'm not feeling you right now. You're too pushy and way too aggressive. The plus side is you're sexy as hell and I admire your confidence."

She moved closer, rubbing her body against mine. "Sexy, confident and truthful. So, for the record, Roc is on my hit list. But I have more than one man on that list. There is, uh, Obama, Daniel Craig, Michael Ealy, Drake, and even my cousin's husband, Rico. All you need to know is that your name sits above all. Start feeling me and make it happen, Jaylin. I'll be ready whenever you are."

She winked and swished her hips from side to side as she walked away. For now, I wasn't impressed. If I was, it was only a little.

I fell asleep with Chase on my mind, but the dream I slipped into was about the love of my life, Nokea. Marriage was the subject, but I was reluctant to go there because I was still bitter about her being with another man.

"Would you please get over it?" She turned my chair around so I could face her. I was at work, trying to put more money into my pockets. Seeing her dressed in a flimsy, colorful dress, looking more and more like Nia Long every day, was very distracting.

"I'm not going to get over it, so back the hell away from me and please exit my office. I can't believe you let that fool take what was mine and do whatever he wished to do with it. I'm not interested in getting married, again, baby. I'm perfectly fine with the way things are."

I got up, causing Nokea to back away from me. I was dressed in a navy business suit and a soft yellow shirt was underneath. Annoyed by her presence, I eased my hands in my pockets and gazed out of the huge picture window in thought. She came up from behind me and secured her arms around my waist. She laid her head against my back and released a deep breath.

"I don't care who you've been with or who I've been with. We always find our way back to each other. I know you're upset about my relationship with Tyrese, but please stop being so unfair. Lord knows I've had to deal with you and plenty of your women for years. But you know what, Jaylin? I don't care anymore. Like you told me before, all of the sex in the world won't wash away your feelings for me. You know that and I do too. So, whenever you put this bitterness behind you, I'm here. Like I've always been. Nothing or no one will ever change that."

I shut my eyes, thinking about why we couldn't seem to get our shit together. Some people did fine with the marriage thing, but unfortunately, we couldn't do it. I felt everything Nokea had said. She always knew how to put me at ease. I turned around to face her, trying my best not to reveal how excited I was to see her.

"Marriage isn't for us," I admitted. "We tried and failed, but—"

She placed her finger on my lips. "I agree. And so what? We still have each other, don't we? At the end of the day, we will always have each other. Papers or no papers, I will always be your wife."

She was trying to sell me this bullshit because she knew I was upset with her. When things were hot and heavy between her and Tyrese, I barely heard from Nokea. She may have come to my office twice, but that was it. Most of the time, I had to call her. We did, however, get our freak on every now and then. Still, it wasn't enough, and I had never been in a predicament where I willingly shared her with another man.

My phone rang, so I went over to my desk to see who was calling. I didn't answer because my eyes were locked on Nokea as she stepped out of her heels, leaving them at the door. She pulled her dress over her head and stood in nothing but a royal blue, silk thong. I didn't want to look at her, so I sat at my desk and opened a drawer to look inside. She could tell I was pretending to be occupied, so she strutted over to my mahogany desk and sat on top of it. She opened her legs right in front of me, causing me to turn my attention away from what was in the drawer.

"Stop being so mean to me." She lifted my chin with her finger and leaned in close, brushing her nose against mine. "You're so handsome when you try to be serious, but I'm determined to put a smile on your face before I leave here."

The direction of my eyes traveled from her pretty pussy lips that swallowed the thong, to her firm breasts that poked out at me. I hoped that she wouldn't notice my dick stretching the fabric in my slacks. It was trying its damndest to get at her. I reached for the papers underneath her.

"Your ass is on some important business proposals. Do you mind?"

Nokea leaned over and lifted her ass so I could remove the papers. After I did, she took the papers from my hand.

"I have a business proposition of my own," she said. "Do you care to hear it?"

"No, *but from this moment on, I don't care to hear anything you have to say, unless it's a moan.*"

Unable to hold back all that I was feeling inside for her, I stood up. Nokea had won this battle for sure and there was no more fight left in me. I leaned in to seal a kiss with her. She tossed the papers over her shoulder and started to unbutton my shirt. I pulled on her thong, ripping it away from her strawberry-scented skin. She wasn't moving fast enough for me, so I hurried to unbuckle my belt and unleashed my hard dick that was just about ready to aim and shoot. But like always in my dreams, when I got ready to crack the code and unlock her pussy, I woke up.

My fist hit the bed. I was upset that my dream hadn't come through for me, but something similar had gone down like that in my office a week before I arrived here. The sex part was out, and I wouldn't allow her to serve me any leftovers. I wished that I could be as forgiving as I was in the dream. There was no doubt that I needed more time to see things her way. For now, Chase may be the one I needed to focus my mind elsewhere. Too aggressive or not, her approach was about to pay off.

Roc

After two more weeks had gone by, I was having Desa Rae withdrawal. I couldn't shake my thoughts about what she had been up to, and I needed to hear her voice. I would give anything right about now to be at home, watching her read one of her favorite books, cooking dinner, or yelling at me for doing or saying the wrong shit. Anything…to have her legs wrapped around my back while fucking her brains out. I could taste her sweetness on my lips. I could feel her sliding up and down on me, and at this point, I felt like I was going whack without her.

I sat at the kitchen table, high as hell from some fire weed Prince had left behind. While in a daze, a vision of Desa Rae's pretty face appeared before me. I saw her at work, handling her business and at home taking care of our daughter. I imagined her tossing and turning in bed, disappointed because I wasn't there. I knew she was missing the hell out of me too, all in the name of Black Love. I don't think I ever loved a woman as much as I loved her, and I hoped like hell that she knew it. Why? Because I was starting to get eager. Eager to get this over with, by any means necessary.

By now, I thought Jeff would've swooped back through here to inquire about a vote. Jaylin and I agreed that Chase had to go. She had started to work her magic on him too. I noticed them getting closer. Their conversation seemed to pick up, and I knew lust in a man's eyes when I saw it.

Me, I was horny as fuck. Jada's thickness was such a turn on to me, but her foul mouth and sassiness made me run far away from her. She probably had some of Li'l Roc's mother, Vanessa's, blood running through her, and that in no way worked for me. I didn't like how bold Chase was, but truthfully, she was the next best thing to a good fuck. I felt myself slipping. That was why I wanted her to hurry up and get out of here.

Lunch was over. After I ended a game of Spades with Jaylin, we changed clothes and went outside to team up for a game of tennis. Nobody really liked to play, but it wasn't as if we had many options. Chase and Jada waited for us to make it to the court. When we got there, it was a pleasure to see them dressed in tight shorts and tanks, and ready to get started. Both of their hair was pulled back into ponytails, but with Chase's being fake, hers hung longer. She rested the racket on her shoulder and squinted at me and Jaylin rocking our tank shirts and shorts.

"How are we going to team up?" Chase asked.

"I say pull names." Jaylin looked at Jada from the corner of his eye. "That way, I don't have to be on nobody's team who ain't willing to work."

Jada rolled her eyes. "Well, looks like you're stuck with me, because Chase thinks she's too cute to play. And you're shit out of luck because I can tell Roc don't know nothin' about playin' tennis."

"You may be right," I said. "But I would put some money on it that you don't know much about it either."

"I know more than you. That's why I prefer to be on Jaylin's team. He always comes off as a real winner."

Jaylin's ego was stroked, so he was down with Jada being on his team. They partnered up on one side; Chase and I were on the other side.

"Who gon' serve the ball first?" I asked.

Jaylin nodded in Chase's direction. She bounced the ball with her racket, then served it over the net. Jada let the ball fly past her, even though it went out of bounds.

"Wait a minute." Jada placed her hand on her hip. "Wasn't Chase supposed to say somethin' like 'one luv'?"

Jaylin responded. "Just do your part in getting the ball over the net, all right?"

Jada rolled her eyes again, and then licked her tongue out at Chase for hitting the ball out of bounds. They thought the shit was funny, but Jaylin and I waited with irritation displayed on our faces for Jada to stop clowning and serve the ball.

"One luv, Jaylin. I bet'cha can't have just one luuuuv," Jada sang.

Jaylin snapped. "Why don't you quit playing so fucking much? Serve the ball. Damn!"

Jada served the ball. It was a decent serve. I hit the ball back over the net and Jaylin followed with a good backhand that dropped in front of Chase. She swung, but missed.

Jada couldn't wait to comment. "She may be cute, but she sho' ain't no Serena Williams. Girl, you swatted that ball like it was a pesky fly."

She and Chase laughed; Jaylin and I didn't. We were ready to get back to the game.

For a while, we had a good routine going, as well as a competitive game. Jada and Jaylin had won the first set and Chase and I were about to win the next one.

"Get yo game face on, Jada," Jaylin suggested. "Come on, baby, let's do this."

"Don't worry about me. I got this."

I served the ball to Jada, thinking that she wasn't on her game. Unfortunately, she was. She hit the ball back over the net and it bounced directly in front of Chase. She swatted at the ball, missing it.

A frown covered my face. "Damn, ma. What you over there doin'? Get focused so we can win this."

"Not today," Jada said. "The way Jaylin's curls over there sweatin', y'all won't be winnin' anything. That brotha is workin' hard. Look at my boo."

She and Chased laughed again; we didn't.

"Do you have a problem with my natural curls?" Jaylin asked Jada.

"No, but why they shinin' and drippin'? They've gotten tighter too, but they still cute, though."

Jaylin tucked the racket underneath his arm and walked over to Jada. "If you help me win this, you can do whatever you wish to with my curls. But now ain't the time to talk about how they look, even though the look of them may be the result of me sweating my ass off while trying to win this game."

"Anything?" Jada wiggled her fingers through his natural curls. "You say I can do anything I wish?"

He grabbed her hand and squeezed her wrist. "Anything. Just not now."

"Okay. Then give me the ball. It's my time to serve, since Chase fell asleep on the last serve and missed."

"No, Chase is getting tired," she said. "I don't like playing tennis, nor do I like that Roc keeps hollering at me."

My face scrunched as I looked in her direction. "Ain't nobody hollerin' at you. I just need for you to pay attention and hit the damn ball."

"See, there you go again. Jada, serve the ball and be sure to hit it toward me."

Jada served the ball. As it came down near Chase, she purposely yawned and ignored it.

"Chase," I shouted. "What the fuck are you doin'?"

"I'm focusing, Roc. Focusing on making us lose this game because you keep yelling at me."

"What the fuck do you want me to do if you ain't puttin' forth no effort to win the game?"

"I want you to apologize to me. Then I may put forth some effort to help *you*."

This shit was a wrap. I was mad as hell. She would get no apology from me, and it was safe to say that Jaylin and Jada had won. If I was forced to say anything else, I would offend Chase. I chalked it up as a loss and kept it moving. I dropped my racket on the ground and held out my fist to give Jada and Jaylin dap for winning.

"Good game," I said. "I guess y'all are the winners by default."

"We'll take it!" Jada shouted.

Jaylin pounded my fist and I cut my eyes at Chase as I headed off the court.

"Fuck you too, Roc," she spat. "I know what that look meant. Instead of acting like a spoiled brat, why don't you man up and say what you really want to say?"

"Ma, you'd better chill with that noise. If I say what I really want to say, you gon' get your feelings hurt. It's best that you pull back and not say another word to me, if you know what's good for you."

"I can't believe you're getting all bent out of shape over a game. Why don't you cheer up? You'll be getting back to that slut you keep mumbling about in your sleep, so cool out."

Chase had touched a nerve. I thought she wouldn't be capable of going there with me, but what did I know? Disrespecting Desa

Rae and calling her a slut was the quickest way to make me show my ass. I cocked my neck from side to side and strutted up to Chase.

"Bitch, you don't know nothin' about me or my woman. My suggestion, correct yourself before I pull a Prince Perkins on that ass. I'mma dare you to say one more offensive thing to me, and I can promise you that doin' so will hurt you more than it will hurt me. Now, make a move with your mouth, if you dare."

As we stood face to face, sucking in the airspace between us, Chase stared at me without a blink. I gazed back into her eyes, watching as they grew with anger. Not once did she open her mouth, but Jaylin did.

"Here we go again, huh? Roc, you know I'm not gon' let you go out like that, so don't even think about it. Chase, apologize to that man and go inside. It's your turn to cook dinner, and after this workout, I'm starving."

For at least another minute, Chase didn't move. She finally blinked and stepped away from me.

"Apology my ass," she mumbled, then walked off. "Jaylin, you need to get some order with your boyz from the hood. They need to learn how to respect the ladies."

"Ladies, I do respect," I fired back. "Hoes, I will not. That's on a for real tip, ma, you've been called out."

I wickedly laughed, watching as Chase and Jada went into the house. The whole damn incident left me with a bad taste in my mouth about Chase. I was going to get my apology, along with so much more than that.

See, Roc had slipped, fell, and bumped his head when he brought up Prince's name like it was a good thing what he had done to me. Didn't he know that women were sensitive about that shit? I was a bit upset with him, but I was sure my anger would cease.

As for the argument between him and Chase, that was a first. He got in her ass over a stupid game, but I was happy to see her stand her ground. I guess since we were the only two females in the house, we had to get along better. The fellas showed how they were willing to come together and boot out Sylvia, so we had to watch our backs.

Now that the tennis game was over, I sat at the computer desk to answer some fan mail that I had gotten. Once I finished replying, I intended to deal with Jaylin and his curls.

Hi, Jada. I'm Shelly P. from Detroit. I gotta say that I almost came looking for you myself when you kept playing with Kiley's heart. I didn't like the way you handled yawl's relationship and you seemed like a real gold-digger. All you did was bitch, bitch, bitch about him and his friends. Why would you try to stop him from being a father to his son? That was wrong on so many levels and I'm glad he finally found somebody who had his back.

See, I was in a good mood, but it was stuff like this that pissed me the fuck off. This surely didn't sound like a fan—more like a hater. I bit into my lip and punched hard on the keyboard to reply.

First of all, Shelly, the only woman who ever had Kiley's back was me. Anna was a fake and he knew it. Sorry that you couldn't see so for yourself. And my heart was the only one being tampered with, because Kiley was trying to live on both sides of the fence. I do, however, regret my childish behavior with his son, but remember that he lied about that too. It was very difficult living with a man and having his friends and family there all the time disrespecting me. You have no idea what that was like, but I put up with it because I loved Kiley to death. His money came in handy, and as a dope-man's woman, was I supposed to run around looking raggedy and shit? Was I supposed to not have my hair and nails done, and not rock the finest clothes that I could? Uh, no. He wanted me to have the best, and I wasn't going to argue with him about that. I'mma end it right here, because you done upset me with yo accusations. The bottom line is I know I contributed to fucking up our relationship, and you already know why I can't change a damn thing that happened. *Tears*

I had to sit for a minute and chill out. Thoughts of Kiley flooded my mind, but after a while, I took a deep breath and stood up. When I walked over to where Jaylin was, he acted like he had forgotten about those curls. I interrupted a boxing match him and Roc were playing on PlayStation, while Chase was cooking dinner.

"What," Jaylin said as I pushed his shoulder.

"Uh, did you forget about your hair? You said I could do anything I wanted to with it."

He ignored me while finishing the boxing game with Roc. When Roc knocked out his character, Jaylin fell back on the couch.

"Damn! I want a do-over. Jada interrupted me and I lost focus."

Roc laughed and stood to stretch. "No excuse. It's over. The rematch has to take place after dinner, because I'm hungry."

"Please tell me why y'all men are so competitive?" I said. "And you may as well sit back down, Roc, because Chase is takin' her sweet little time in the kitchen."

Roc looked into the kitchen, seeing that there wasn't much going on. He sat back down and relaxed on the couch.

"What is it that you're trying to do with my hair?" Jaylin questioned.

"I'm not sure yet. I'm thinkin' like maybe shavin' some of it off or straightenin' it. I really want to see you with a baldhead or with straight hair."

His eyes widened. "My suggestion would be that you come up with another idea. My hair does not straighten and a baldhead doesn't work for me."

"Excuse me, mister, but you said that I could do anything. You also been around here braggin' about how you're a man of your word and what you say, you mean. Are you backtrackin' now?"

"I'm not backtracking at all. You just need to come up with other suggestions."

"You seriously got a problem with lettin' people have their way, don't you? I tell you what, though. If you let me straighten your hair, I'll shave my puddy hairs and cook breakfast, lunch, and dinner for you, for the next three days."

"No deal. For starters, your cooking ain't all that to me, and your puddy hairs should already be shaved. But if you let Chase wax your hairs and allow her to suck you in front of me, then we may have a deal."

I couldn't help but to frown as him and Roc high-fived each other. "Ugh, that's nasty. I don't get down like that, but you can watch Roc suck it. Somethin' tells me he'll do a much better job than Chase."

"You got that shit right," Roc said. "And I'll shave it for you, too."

I smiled from the thought of him going down on me. How nice of him to offer. This was getting interesting. I took a seat on the coffee table; it had the nerve to squeak. Jaylin had to go there.

"You need to back off those tables," he said. "I don't want a repeat of the other night, so please sit on the couch."

I threw my hand back at him and remained on the table. "Forget you. I'm stayin' right here, so listen up. I'mma go in the closet and get this perm I got from Big Lots. I'm gon' straighten your hair and knock out some of those curls. Then, you gon' shave me and we both gon' have the pleasure of watchin' Roc perform oral sex on me. How about that?"

Roc looked at Jaylin, but he seemed more interested in his curls. "Why are you so eager to mess with my curls? My hair is natural, baby. You will never get my hair to go straight. In addition to that, what in the hell is Big Lots? Never heard of that before."

"That's because you've been sheltered for too long. People who have maids don't know nothin' about Big Lots. The perm I got will straighten your hair. I do love your hair, but I think it may look so much better slicked back with some gel on it. You know, some of that gangsta shit, baby. Especially since you're a pimp anyway. It's time that you represent."

"I'm already representing myself in a major way and no adjustments will be needed," Jaylin said. "But, since I am a man of my word, do whatever. Again, my hair will not go straight. You're going to be disappointed, but you still gotta live up to your end of the bargain. I'd rather see Chase do you, and I won't be satisfied until it's done."

Roc added his two cents. "I'm kind of leanin' that way as well, but I'm more eager to see you put a perm in this nigga's hair. Somethin' tells me that he ain't got no idea what a relaxer will do."

I stood and reached for Jaylin's soft hair to rub it. "Well, we're about to see. Are we not?"

He snatched his head back and cut his eyes. "Only one side, Jada. Sample that shit before you put it all over my head, and let me see if it has any effects."

I rushed out of the living room and yelled into the kitchen at Chase. "Hurry up with that food, girl! How much longer we got?"

"At least another thirty minutes," she said, huffing and looking like a confused bitch who needed to exit the kitchen fast. "I know you're not about to do what I think."

"Yes, ma'am. I'm goin' to get my perm now."

Chase laughed and shook her head. I hurried to the closet before Jaylin changed his mind. I couldn't believe he was going to let me do this, but when I returned to the living room area, he took the relaxer box from my hand.

"What the hell is a relaxer? Is it supposed to relax me?"

"All its gon' do is wave your hair more," Roc said, lying. "I don't know why Jada so hyped about puttin' that shit in your hair."

Chase had already made her way to the living room to see what was up. "I don't suspect it's going to do anything either. You can't straighten natural curls."

Jaylin gave the box back to me. "Wash my hair first. It's still sweaty from earlier."

He made his way to the kitchen, and when I looked at Chase and Roc, they had smirks on their faces. They definitely knew what time it was. This fool was about to burn.

"Come on, sweetie," I said to Jaylin as he stood by the sink. "I'm goin' to get a bath towel and some shampoo."

He waited until I returned with the towel and shampoo. By then, he had his shirt off, displaying his perfectly carved chest. His shorts hung low and his bulge always made it appear that he was hard and ready. I swear I wanted to drop to my knees or bend the fuck over in front of him. Either way, I couldn't go wrong.

As soon as he bent over and put his head underneath the faucet, I squeezed the shampoo in my hand and got to work.

"That feels guuud," Jaylin moaned as I massaged my fingers in his hair, washing it. He had a good grade of healthy hair. I hoped the perm wouldn't fuck it up too bad. I seriously couldn't believe he was going to let me do this, but I guess it said a lot about him keeping his word. I now felt better about the money he said he'd give me, if I won this challenge.

Chase came into the kitchen to check on the baked chicken she had in the oven.

"Almost done," she said. "You and Jaylin need to hurry up and get out of the kitchen, especially while I'm trying to cook. Couldn't you have done that in the bathroom?"

I ignored Chase's comment, but whispered for her to come by me and Jaylin.

"Move his shorts," I whispered to her.

She chuckled and didn't hesitate to reach her hand inside of his shorts.

"What you doing, Jada?" Jaylin turned his head to the side. His eyes were closed because of the dripping shampoo and water. I kept on massaging his hair while Chase massaged something else.

"My hands are in your hair," I said. "I don't know what you're referrin' to."

"You know damn well what I'm referrin' to."

"Aw, that. Roc, please get your hands off that man's nuts so I can finish washin' his hair."

Jaylin jumped up and backed away from the sink. His face was drenched with shampoo and water dripping down it. So was his chest, but the most exciting part to see was his hard dick poking through his shorts.

Chase and I stood like two innocent angels who hadn't done a thing. Roc walked by the kitchen, shaking his head. "I know you didn't think my hands were on yo shit, did you?"

"No, I didn't, but I jumped up because somebody was about to get a handful of sperm."

Jaylin winked at Chase. For whatever reason, I didn't like it. He was starting to give her way too much attention. She loved every bit of it.

"The pleasure would've been all mine," she said. "Maybe next time, huh?"

"Next time," Roc said, turning to walk away. "Keep me out of it. I'm gettin' ready to wash some clothes. Chase, before you touch my food, be sure to wash your hands."

I guess he was still hot with Chase from earlier. His tone said so. Or it probably bothered him that Chase was now riding Jaylin's dick. She had been riding it all along, but more so within the past week. I had to keep my eyes on this trick for sure.

I threw the towel over Jaylin's head, watching as he took his time tucking the monster back into his shorts.

"You proud of that bad boy, ain't you?" I teased. "Just lettin' it all hang out. But, uh, now that I'm done washin' your hair, go have a seat on the couch so I can get this party started."

Jaylin put the towel around his neck, cocking it from side to side. "Jada, do you think I'm a fool or a damn fool? Baby, I'm not about to let you put no five-dollar perm from a place called Big Lots in my hair. I'm not about to let you cut it either, so whatever plans you had for me, you can forget it. I needed my hair washed, so thanks for doing it for me."

He kissed my cheek and left me shaking my head. "Oooo, you

are dir-tee. I thought you were a man of your word. Shame on you for gettin' me hyped about this."

"I am a man of my word, and when I say that you're not fucking with my hair, I mean it. Again, thanks for washing it for me. I needed that. Needed something else too."

That comment was addressed to Chase and she blushed. As Jaylin walked away, I could tell things were getting pretty serious. I guess it was my fault for asking her to play with him. I didn't expect for her to do that good of a job, and it surprised me that she was starting to win him over. Bitch.

I was so mad that, immediately after dinner, I got ready for bed early. I also couldn't stop thinking about that email I'd gotten earlier about Kiley. It was heavy on my mind. I fell asleep dreaming about men.

"There's Some Whores in This House" was playing in the background, and Jaylin stood in front of the bed with no clothes on, doing the percolator. A serious look was washed across his face, but his eyes were narrow as they zoned in on me with seduction. A bag of green grapes was in my hand. I chomped down on them, refusing to turn my eyes in another direction. Jaylin had me hooked, and his dick was hanging close to his knees.

"I'm a ho, you know I'm a ho. How do you know? Because I showed you so," he said.

"Yes, you've been representin' very well, so keep on hoein' and turn around so I can see how you doin' it from the back."

Jaylin stopped percolating and turned around. He stuck his dick between his legs, causing one of the grapes to drop from my wide opened mouth. I was on cloud nine, ten, and eleven, and when the direction of my eyes shifted to the right of Jaylin, I saw Roc twirling around on a stripper pole. With no clothes on, he was grinding the hell out of the pole while smacking his ass. I wanted to get out of the bed to go touch him and

Jaylin, but for whatever reason, I couldn't move. I had to wait for them to come to me.

Minutes later, they did. Both of them crawled on the bed, and when Roc growled at me, I growled back. He snatched the grapes from my hand, causing me to frown.

"What are you doin'?" I pouted. "I want my grapes back."

"But you're too fat, ma. You don't need them."

No this motherfucker didn't just go there. I snatched my bag of grapes from his hand and started eating more of them. Roc tried to make it up to me by rubbing my legs and Jaylin picked up a few of the grapes, popping them into my mouth. Juice from the grapes squirted on his face and all he did was laugh.

"I love juice, but you can give me much more than that," he said.

He attempted to pull my nightgown over my head, but for a minute, it got stuck. Roc yanked on it and tossed it on the bed beside us. It was the first time I'd ever let any man see my entire naked body, and they seemed pleased by how voluptuous it was.

"You get the front," Jaylin said to Roc. "I'll get the back."

I happily lay sideways and they made a thick sandwich out of me.

"Did anybody bring any mayonnaise or mustard?" I asked.

Jaylin reached behind him and brought forth a jar of Grey Poupon. "Forget the mustard, let's settle for the Grey Poupon."

We released a hearty laugh, but Jaylin couldn't get the jar open. He passed it to Roc and he couldn't get it open either.

"Forget it," Roc said. "She didn't need it anyway."

Roc's insults were working me, and since he was in front of me, I let him have it. I sucked his thick lips and lowered my hand to touch his package. Unfortunately, it was so small—felt like it melted in my hands.

"What in the hell am I supposed to do with this?" I asked.

"Anything you want to. Just don't eat it, fatty."

I pushed Roc on the floor, tossing him out of the picture. Jaylin, how-

ever, was still behind me. He threw my leg over his and whispered sweet nothings in my ear.

"You're so fucking fine, Jada. I want this pussy, baby, give me all of it."

By now, I was hot and sho'nuff bothered. Jaylin's whole hand was cupped over my pussy, and as he started to finger me, I sucked in a heap of air.

"You really need to shave, baby, and the sharp nails on your toes are cutting my leg. I don't understand why a woman as beautiful as you are won't take care of herself."

"I will," I replied. "Just be sure to give me all of your money, and I will look better than any bitch you ever laid your eyes on."

"Not a chance in hell," Roc said, peeking over the bed. I shooed that hater away like a pesky fly, and right before Jaylin was getting ready to hit me with his snake, the bedroom door flew open. In walked Kiley, surrounded by a white light. The room fell silent and an orchestra appeared, playing R. Kelly's, "When a Woman Loves a Man." Kiley was naked too, and all of these big dicks in the room made me nervous. I had been caught red-handed in the bed with Jaylin, and Kiley didn't like it one bit. His bald head was sweating and his fists were tightened. His eyes had turned red and his buffed chest heaved in and out.

"Bitch, what you doin'?" he yelled. "How many niggas am I gon' catch you in the bed with?"

"Ju...just one," I said, easing away from Jaylin.

He reached for my hand, trying to stop me from moving away from him. "Baby, don't go. I need you right now. I thought we were in this shit together, and you know how I feel about you, don't you?"

I batted my lashes, wanting to cry. But the way Kiley was looking at me, I wouldn't dare shed one tear. To show him how sorry I was, I dropped to my knees and prepared myself to give him head. That would surely put a smile on his face, but Jaylin and Roc weren't too happy.

"Don't do it," Jaylin said softly. "Baby, please don't do it. If you do, save some for me."

"Gon' ahead and let that ho do her thing," Roc spat. "All she gon' do is bite that shit anyway."

I'd just about had it with Roc, and as I stood to go after him, the door opened again. Prince strutted into the room. He was also naked. It was now time for me to wake the hell up before something popped off that I didn't want to.

"Get out! Now!" I shouted to Prince.

"Why should I leave when I hear there's a head hunter in here? You got plenty mo brothas outside of that door waitin', so you need to speed up yo game and get busy."

They all laughed and charged toward me. I screamed "no," and that was when I jumped out of my dream.

I sat up in bed with a heaving chest. Roc was lying next to me sound asleep. Jaylin was sitting up in his bed with the nightlight on, reading. He was in his boxer shorts and the book was propped up in front of his dick.

"What in the hell is wrong with you?" he asked.

I squeezed my achy forehead. "Nothin'. Just had a bad dream, that's all."

He ignored me and got back to reading his book. I wasn't sure where Chase was, but that was one messed up dream. I couldn't even go back to sleep. I lay there wondering what the purpose was for all of that foolishness.

"Say, Jaylin. Do you like grapes?"

All he did was stare at me, and then his eyes returned to the book. Oh well, I suspected he didn't like grapes. I reminded my-self to ask Roc the same question later.

Chase

I needed an A for effort and an A-plus for succeeding at making Jaylin feel differently about me. I didn't care what anybody said. The most powerful, rich, handsome, spiritual, and successful men on this earth could be brought down by the power of one thing. I knew that thing to be pussy.

I pretty much knew I'd have my work cut out for me with Jaylin, but my aggressive approach was well worth it. Roc, on the other hand, he was mad at me right now, but he'd soon be singing a new tune.

To me, it wasn't that much love one could have for another, particularly love for the woman Roc had been in a daze about. While no one was looking, I was doing my research. I saw several pictures of Desa Rae tucked inside of his sweat-suit jacket. There was another picture of the two of them with their daughter. There was something about Desa Rae that was interesting to me, so I dug further. I found out that she and Roc were engaged. She was much older than he was, she had a darn good job, and she lived in an upscale neighborhood outside of St. Louis. She was divorced, had a son who had recently graduated from college, and she was considered a plus-sized woman.

Nowhere near as cute as I was, she still had it going on. I understood Roc's attraction to her. What I didn't understand was his love that was holding him back. Of course I was upset with him about how he'd spoken to me during the tennis game, but my anger with him had been stirring way before then. I didn't like being rejected. I felt as if we had too many opportunities to get down and dirty with each other. I had put myself out there way too much, so at this point, I was considering blackmail. Not because I was interested in a relationship with Roc, but simply because I took issue with men who teased me. From day one, that was all he'd been doing. One day he'd be up, the next day down. He needed to stop pretending that he was so in love with Desa Rae. And more than anything, I saw his flirting as pure disrespect to me. It was also an insult, especially if he wasn't serious about hooking up for real.

Pertaining to the blackmail thingy, I didn't have access to any cameras or cell phones where I could take pictures of him in the act doing something inappropriate. I wasn't even sure if Desa Rae would trip, but what did I have to lose? In the end, I'd have a piece of her man and she'd have a headache.

As for Jaylin, don't think for one minute that I didn't do my homework on him. He was a piece of work, so I wasn't about to touch the madness he had going on. There were too many women— baby's mamas, a wife, several mistresses, Facebook companions, too many kids—but a whole lot of damn money. With him, what you see is what you get. I couldn't believe how much he was worth, but his money wasn't what I was interested in. A good fuck would do me fine—case closed.

At two in the morning, I sat in the living room by myself thinking and watching TV. Everyone else was asleep, or so I thought until Jada came out of the bedroom. Dressed in an oversized T-

shirt for pajamas and a scarf tied around her head, she sluggishly made her way to the kitchen. I wasn't sure if she saw me or not, until she snatched a bag of cheese puffs from the closet and turned around.

"Shoot," she said, coming into the living room and plopping down on the couch. "I got hungry. I couldn't sleep for nothin', and my stomach kept on grumblin'. I need a loxative or somethin'."

I didn't bother to correct her; those days were long gone. If she didn't care about her incorrect usage of words, neither did I.

"I don't know if those cheese puffs are going to help your stomach. You may want to try something like a banana or some yogurt."

"No, thank you. I'll stick to my cheese puffs and figure out my bowels later. Meanwhile, what you doin' up so late?"

"I'm watching a good movie on cable. I also had a lot on my mind and couldn't sleep."

"Like what?"

"You know, like what's up with this house. I wonder how all of it will end. I also have some ideas in my head to make it end sooner. I guess my question for you is what's your take on all of this? What do you expect to gain and how serious are you about being the last person here? More than anything, are you staying for the money?"

Jada didn't hesitate. "You're damn right I'm here for the money. Ain't you?"

"At first I was. Now, I'm not so sure."

"Then, why else would you stick around? If it's not for the money, then you may as well leave."

"No, I don't want to leave. I'm kind of enjoying myself here. Roc and Jaylin are a trip. I'm intrigued by both of them."

"I am too, but I'm more intrigued by winnin' that money."

I paused for a moment to look at the TV. Truthfully, I was in deep thought again. "Let me ask you another question, Jada. Is there any way possible that, if I win, we can split the money? Or if you win we'll split it?"

"No, ma'am, I'm sorry, there ain't. I remember how it went down in that movie with Larenz Tate playin' Frankie Lymon. He had all them wives, and after they agreed to split the money, Vivica Fox wound up takin' the money and runnin'. Women can't be trusted, and you know that I ain't got no reason to trust you."

"No you don't, but I guess that's something I'll have to earn over time."

"Good luck with that." Jada stood up. "I'm goin' to the bathroom, then I'm goin' back to bed. I had a weird-ass dream. Do you know what it means when you find yourself caught up in a bedroom with four men?"

"It means that you're a freak with some serious sexual desires."

"I don't know about all of that, but let me tell you what happened in my dream."

Jada started telling me about her dream. I cracked up and covered my mouth in disbelief. What kind of person had a dream like that? I couldn't even picture Jaylin dancing to that song and begging her to be with him. Nor could I visualize Roc swinging on a pole and smacking his ass.

"Were the grapes sweet?" I jokingly asked. "That was too funny."

"The grapes were real sour, but, girl, the men showed up and showed out in my dream. Do you think I should tell them about it?"

"No, Jada, please no. They would think you're out of your mind."

"That's what I figured. By the time Prince showed up, I was happy to get out of there. I started runnin' for the door and they all came after me. Even the men in the orchestra chased me."

"Wow. I don't know what to say about that dream. The message behind it is so confusing. Have you had sex with a lot of men?"

Jada looked up, seeming to be in thought. "Not really, but I don't know what you might consider a lot of men. I'm sure I haven't had more than you, but I could probably count the number of men I've had on both hands."

"Well, good for you. Believe it or not, I could probably do the same."

Jada stretched and yawned. "Just so you know, I don't believe you, 'cause you come across as a woman who done had a lot of experience with dick. No offense, I'm just sayin'."

"And I'm sayin' that it hasn't been as many as you think. I'm picky and it takes a lot for a man to get this. Trust me on that."

Jada wasn't buying it, but I didn't care. More than anything, I used men to get what I wanted. Sometimes it revolved around sex, and sometimes it didn't.

"Whatever you say. I'll see you in the mornin'. If I feel up to it, I'mma cook us some omelets filled with sausage, bacon, ham, and cheese. You and Jaylin ole funny actin' selves can eat whatever. Roc and me gon' throw down."

"I love omelets too, so count me in."

Jada nodded, then left the living room. She spent about twenty minutes in the bathroom, and after she finished, I went in. I sprayed Lysol and quickly changed into a turquoise lace nightgown that showed my goodies. I moisturized my skin with Forever Red lotion from Bath & Body Works, and then I stepped into a pair of comfortable house shoes. Afterward, I left the bathroom and went out back to entertain the man who had been giving me all of the information I needed, especially since I was forced to switch to Plan B.

"You look awesome," Jeff said with pure lust in his eyes. He wrapped his arms around me. "I've been dying to see you again."

"It's a good thing the wait is over."

I took the envelope with more information in it from his hand. He followed me to a cozy spot in the far back of the game room. As he sat on the couch, I stood in front of him, touching myself. My nightgown hit the floor and his eyes scanned me from head to toe.

"I want you to hurry up and leave here, Chase. I don't know how much more of this sneaking around stuff I can do. It's been no picnic watching you with Jaylin and Roc. I'd be lying to you if I said I wasn't a little jealous."

A jealous man couldn't even get it, but Jeff was sitting on too much information that I needed to win this challenge. He was willing to do just about anything for me, and with him being in charge of this whole thing, I could already taste victory.

"Be patient," I said. "Doing so will benefit both of us, and remember that Jaylin and Roc are only part of the plan. I need your help with this. When all is said and done, we will be able to spend as much time together as you want us to."

I stepped forward and straddled Jeff's lap. He loved to suck my breasts and his hands roamed all over them.

He removed his curled tongue from my tiny, hard nipple and looked up at me. "What about Jada, sweetheart? Are you concerned about her at all?"

"Not one bit. She's a loser, so ignore anything that she does around here. I'm going to use her to take care of a few things for me. Then she'll be sent packing like everyone else. Now, if you don't mind, my breasts kind of liked the attention you were giving them. Please resume. Let's save the questions for another time, especially since I've waited all day for this."

Jeff smiled, but my smile was forced. I had to stroke his ego, and I knew that one fuck up from me could turn this whole thing around. He could easily turn his back on me. I didn't want that to happen, so I was determined to put something heavy on his mind.

He leaned in and took tiny bites on my lips. He didn't even know how to grip my ass the right way, and I would bet any amount of money that Roc wouldn't have a problem with it. I erased the thoughts of him from my head and laid Jeff back on the couch. I helped to remove his clothes and laughed to myself at the size of his package. In no way was it capable of satisfying me, but I pretended that it was the best. Jeff was my ticket to pulling myself out of debt. And if this wasn't proof that a woman could get anything she wanted, I'd be happy to say it again. Never, ever underestimate the power of pussy. Well, not mine for sure.

Jaylin

I was getting real pissed at how messy this house was. I figured everybody got tired of me complaining, but so damn what. If they didn't want to hear my mouth, then it was in their best interest to start cleaning up after themselves. What may not have been nasty to them was too nasty to me. It was as if nobody gave a care that dust was starting to build up on the furniture or that the floors had lost their shine. Then there was the kitchen where dishes had been left overnight. If there was a dishwasher in the house, how or why wasn't it being used?

As far as the bedroom was concerned, forget it. Nobody made their beds, clothes were left on the floor, and the smell of funky socks permeated the air.

The most irritating thing of all was the bathroom. Soap scum didn't work for me and neither did hair follicles in and around the toilet. The mirrors were smudged and these fools didn't even take time to put toilet paper on the roll.

Even the patio, game room, and workout room were a mess. Used towels were here and there, and who in the fuck would drink something and leave their glass on the table? At this point, I wasn't eating much, touching nothing, or sitting my ass on anything unless I cleaned it myself.

With an attitude, I whipped up a quick fruit salad while the others ate omelets. Once I was done, I went outside to eat and read the newspaper. I wasn't out there two minutes before Chase decided to join me.

"I figured you wouldn't eat those omelets Jada made, but from me to you, they were pretty darn good."

"From me to you, I don't put stuff like that in my body. But thanks for the update."

Chase looked up and squinted at the sun. At eight in the morning, it was already scorching hot outside. "It looks like a great day to relax in the pool. After breakfast, would you like to join me? I'll give you a nice massage and rub your entire body with some of my special oils."

"Sounds like a plan. But first, let me call Jeff to see what's up with the maid service I inquired about. Then I need to check with Roc to see if he wants to finish the boxing game we started yesterday. I'll let you know what's up after that."

Chase nodded, then drank her apple juice. Minutes later, Jada came outside dancing with a plate in her hand. Half of her omelet was on it and several slices of toast were beside it. If dancing wasn't enough, she started singing.

"I've got jungle fever, he's got jungle fever, she's got jungle fever, we've all got jungle fever— Don't we, Chase?"

Chase gagged and spit some of the apple juice from her mouth. "Wha…what are you talking about, Jada?"

Jada slapped Chase hard on her back, causing her jerk forward. "You know what I'm talkin' about. Don't play."

Chase appeared confused. "I, uh, don't know, but it's nobody's business if I date white men. Is that what you're getting at?"

Jada winked at her. "That and a whole lot more. I also date white men, so it ain't no biggie. I wonder if Jaylin dates white women. Do you Jaylin?"

"Why is it that every time we out here chilling, y'all start asking me questions about my personal life? Who I date doesn't matter. What matters is how y'all been fucking up and haven't been keeping the house clean. Is it that hard, ladies, for y'all to pick up after yourselves?"

"No," Jada said, chewing her food. "But why should we clean when you around here actin' like you're employed by Merry Maids? My towels do not have to be neatly folded on the towel rack, my house shoes do not need to be placed beside my bed, my bed does not need to be made up in the mornin', and my panties don't have to be ironed. I guess you'll be ironin' those next, but please leave my stuff alone. In due time, I'll put my stuff where it needs to be."

Chase defended her actions as well. "She's right, Jaylin. What you do is a bit much. This house is not dirty at all. With four people living here, some things are to be expected."

I couldn't believe what they were saying to me. "I'm speechless. After y'all get done eating, please get up and follow me."

Jada put her plate on the table and stood up. "I'm done with my plate. That was my second one and I'm full. You have my attention, so where are we goin?"

Chase stood and both of them followed me into the house. We passed by Roc, who was sitting at the kitchen table eating with headsets on, listening to music. I stopped in the living room first, and swiped my finger across the top of the TV, the bookshelves and the table. A pile of dust was on my finger.

"What's up with this?" I said. "What does it look like?"

"It looks like some dust bunnies are tryin' to find a place to lay.

Besides, you swiped your finger in three different places. If that's all the dust you got, then what you complainin' for?"

"I agree," Chase said. "It wasn't that much, Jaylin, and you can find way more dust than that in my living room at home."

"I'm sure I would, and your comment doesn't surprise me one bit. Follow me."

They followed me into the bathroom. The first thing that I pointed out was the hair follicles on and around the toilet.

Jada gasped and put her hand close to her mouth. "Oh. My. God! That toilet is filthy! But, uh, I don't see anything. What are you talkin' about?"

"Right there, Jada. I'm not going to touch it, but you see that hair on the toilet."

"One strand," Chase said. "I see one little strand that I almost need a magnifying glass to see."

"You don't need a magnifying glass to see that hair. All you need is some sense. It's hair all over that toilet. Weren't you supposed to clean the bathroom yesterday?"

Chase folded her arms in front of her. "I did clean it, and I did a great job doing so."

"I'm glad you think so." I swiped my finger along the scum on the glass shower doors. "If you cleaned the bathroom yesterday, then why is there soap scum on the glass?"

"Jaylin, you need to quit," Jada said. "I hope this maid service hurry up and get here, because you are workin' my nerves with this mess. It ain't that much cleanin' in the world. You need to realize that some people don't clean bathrooms with a toothbrush like you do."

"Some people don't clean at all. I'm done griping about this, but when roaches start trying to go to bed with y'all, don't come running to me."

I left the bathroom in a hurry so I could email Jeff to see what was up with the maid service I had recommended. He sent me an email back right away, telling me that someone would be here today. Thank God.

After I read his email, I checked my fan mail. There was plenty of it, but one message in particular caught my attention, so I responded to Evelyn Walters from Los Angeles.

Hello, Mr. Naughty Man. Like many people, I have followed your story since the very beginning. And needless to say, I can't get enough of you. You've had me on an emotional rollercoaster, and I'm not quite ready to get off yet. I get upset with the women in your life for staying with you, but then I find myself mad at them for not giving you what you want. I do understand how difficult it is for them to pull themselves away from you, because here I am reading about you and I can't let go. My question is what do you think it is that makes Jaylin Rogers so addictive?

I must have answered this question over a thousand times, but it was a question that always put a smile on my face.

Evelyn, the easy answer to your question would be the love for my dick, but I must give women more credit than that. Nobody falls head over heels for me because of that, and I reject the notion that any woman stays with me because she is solely in love with my skills in the bedroom. Over the course of many years, it has been a combination of things that makes women intrigued by me. My honesty, confidence, good looks, charm, intelligence, and ability to please the pussy, all of those things work together in my favor. The good thing is I like to spread love whenever I can. So, I hope your addiction lasts for quite some time. I'm always delighted to add another set of panties to my collection, especially if they're clean. Stay sweet, Miss Naughty, and holla back later. Peace.

I logged off the computer, and later that day, I was shooting the breeze with Roc in the living room when the maid service finally decided to show up. I could see the van parked in the driveway.

When I opened the door, there stood a decent-looking black woman with a bucket filled with cleaning materials in her hand. The second she laid her eyes on me, her face fell flat. I wasn't sure why, until I put two and two together, realizing who she was.

"Brittany?" I said, opening the door for her to come inside.

"No, it's Brashaney, Jaylin. It doesn't surprise me that you forgot my name."

I smiled, attempting to knock off some of the attitude she displayed. After all, I had forgotten her name, yet I needed her services today.

"I knew what your name was, woman. I was only kidding."

"I don't believe that for one minute, but it's good seeing you again. It's been a long time. I see you haven't changed much."

"Neither have you."

I checked her out. She had much ass squeezed into a pair of tight jeans that looked painted on, a white, button-down smock with "Time To Come Clean" was embroidered on the pocket and her hair was in a layered, short cut. Her brown skin was smooth and flawless. I couldn't help but to look at her nails. Back in the day, I had to dismiss her because the polish on her nails was messy and chipped. And an outfit she'd worn one day was not suitable for the black-tie event I invited her to, so I had to call her out on it. I wondered if she was still upset about that or if she even remembered. I damn sure wasn't going to bring it up. If she did, I intended to play clueless.

As she stood in the foyer, I closed the door. She looked around, then put the bucket on the floor.

"This is a nice place, but it's kind of a downgrade for you, isn't it?"

Jeff told me not to provide any information about Hell House to the maid service. Their job was to come here and clean. Nothing more, nothing less.

"This isn't my house, but I'm staying here for a while. Just need you to work your magic up in here, if you know what I mean."

"By the looks of things, there doesn't seem like much to do. But I'll do my best. If you need for me to pay more attention to certain areas, please let me know."

"I can tell you right now that the bathroom needs extra cleaning and so does the kitchen. Dust the whole house, and the floors are kind of jacked up. Did you bring some help with you?"

"No, I didn't. I should be able to handle this. I'm used to doing this."

"How long do you think it'll take you?"

"A few hours or so. Maybe longer."

"If you need my help with anything, let me know."

Brashaney said that she didn't need my help, and she left to get a few more items from the truck. My mind was traveling a mile a minute. I tried to remember every single detail of what had happened between us. At this point, I couldn't even remember if the pussy was worth bragging about or not. That was on my mind because when she came back into the house, Roc's eyes were all over her.

"Say, ma. Let me know if you need some help when you start cleanin' the bedroom," he joked.

Brashaney blushed and extended her hand to him. "If I wasn't working, I would consider your offer. But my name is Brashaney. Yours?"

"Roc. Roc Dawson."

"Nice to meet you. My boss told me that the client was pretty anxious to get this house cleaned, so I'd better get started. Besides, I don't want to disappoint anyone."

She glanced at me, and then walked off to get busy.

Roc sat on the couch and so did I. He picked up a cigar he'd been puffing on earlier and lit it. "She's dope," he said. "Real sweet."

I put my hands behind my head and placed my foot on the edge of the table. "No doubt, but she also got an anger problem too."

It came back to me that she kicked my Mercedes when I asked her to leave my house one day. I couldn't remember why, but there were several instances where she was upset with me.

Roc blew smoke from his mouth. "Do you know her?"

"We used to holla. Nothing on a serious tip. Just a few occasions where we shook things up in the bedroom."

Roc snickered. "Was it good?"

"Can't remember."

"Then it wasn't."

"I may have to agree."

Roc laid the cigar in the ashtray and picked up the controller so we could continue our basketball game. Shortly thereafter, Jada and Chase came in from outdoors. They'd been outside all morning, trying to get tanned while chilling by the pool.

"It's so nice outside," Chase said. "Are the two of you going to join us or are y'all going to sit in here all day playing video games?"

"I'll be out later," Roc replied. "This game got me on lock right now."

We all looked up when we saw Brashaney making her way down the hallway with a duster in her hand. She had on headphones while dusting the baseboards and pictures on the walls.

"Who dis' big-booty woman, Harpo?" Jada put her hand on her hip. "And when they start sendin' maids to people's houses with tight-ass jeans on?"

"I know, right." With jealousy in her eyes, Chase checked out Brashaney. "I'm used to maids being old with wrinkles. I guess tricks out there struggling must do what they have to do to make some money."

Jada continued on. "With that big ass, she may be better off on a stripper pole."

Her and Chase laughed and kept on talking about Brashaney. I didn't say a word. It didn't surprise me that they were going in on her. I got back to my game with Roc, until Brashaney came into the room and removed her headphones.

"Hello, ladies," she said with a welcoming smile. Chase and Jada waved, then turned their attention back to the fashion magazine they were paging through.

"I so want those shoes." Chase pointed to a picture in the magazine. "But they cost too much."

Brashaney cleared her throat. I assumed that she noticed the attitude as well. "Hey, Jaylin. Would you do me a favor and get the vacuum cleaner out of my truck? It's kind of heavy."

I paused the game and left to go get the vacuum cleaner for Brashaney. I was gone for only five minutes, but when I got back, Chase and Jada were looking at me, shaking their heads. Brashaney was standing next to them with a raised brow.

"What?" I questioned.

"You know what," Brashaney said. "Let's just say that I had an opportunity to shed a little light on our past relationship."

"Relationship? I don't recall that we had one."

Jada laughed and stood up. "On that note, I'm goin' to the bathroom." She looked at Brashaney. "I hope you're not comin' in there anytime soon, because I got some demons to release. My stomach has been bubblin' and boilin' all mornin'."

"No need to announce it," I said, frowning. "Just go handle your business."

Jada rushed out of the room holding her stomach. I told Brashaney the vacuum cleaner was by the door, and for the next several hours she got busy. Real busy—I must say so myself, especially since I went behind her to make sure things were done the right way. She didn't wrap it up until almost nine o'clock that night. I stood at the door, wrapping the cord around the vacuum cleaner so I could take it back to the truck.

"Thank you," she said, wiping sweat from her forehead and drinking from a glass of cold lemonade that I had given to her.

"No, thank you. I appreciate this, and you can be sure that I'll be calling for you again real soon."

"I hope so. This is the most money that I've made all week. Plus, I enjoyed myself. It was good seeing you and it was quite a surprise."

"Same here." I reached out to give her a hug. She held on real tight—so tight that it made me wonder what she was feeling inside. I backed away from her, then kissed her cheek.

"I'mma take this outside," I said, referring to the vacuum cleaner. "Do you need my help with anything else?"

"I do, but I'll settle for another glass of lemonade."

"Go ahead in the kitchen and tell Roc to get you some more. I'll be outside."

She nodded and walked away. As I was straightening the items in the truck so I could put the vacuum cleaner in it, Brashaney came outside. She waited until I was done before reaching out for another hug.

I couldn't help but to question her demeanor. "What's up with all of this? Is everything good with you?"

This time, she backed away from me. "Of course. Like I said, it was good seeing you. Take care of yourself, Jaylin, and be good."

"I'll try, but you know me."

We laughed. I watched as she got in the truck and left. Afterward, I went back inside, thinking about the strange look in her eyes. Something was definitely bugging her. Since she didn't say anything, I didn't think much more of it. That was until nearly two hours later, when I was getting ready to call it a night. I had spent some quiet time in the pool with Chase and was on my way into the bedroom where Jada and Roc were sitting on the bed playing cards. The doorbell rang, and after Roc went to the door, he told me that someone was looking for me.

I pointed to my chest, then placed the towel around my neck, after I dried off. "Who, me? Somebody is at the door for me?"

Roc nodded. "Yep. It's that chick who was here earlier."

I went to the door and saw Brashaney standing on the porch. This time, her SUV was in the driveway, instead of the work truck. Before I asked why she was there, I invited her inside.

"Thanks," she said, looking up at the cloudy sky. "It looks like it's about to start raining and thundering."

"Yeah, they mentioned something like that in the forecast, but what's up? What brings you back here?"

She started to fidget She rubbed her hands together and could barely look me in the eyes. "Is there somewhere we can talk in private? I know it's late, but I really need to say a few things to you."

I wasn't sure what all of this was about, so I invited her to have a seat in the front room that was right off the foyer. So far, none of us had utilized the small room, per Jeff's request. She took a seat on the sofa and I sat in a chair next to it.

Silence soaked the room for a minute, then she released a deep breath. She reached over to touch my hands that were clenched together. "First, let me say, again, that it was so good seeing you today. Over the years, I thought so much about how things went down with us. I have so many regrets. Like you said today, we never really had a relationship or anything like that, but I was so hurt when I came to your house that night and saw you getting out of the car with that other woman."

My memory wasn't about nothing. I sat there trying to remember who the hell she was talking about, then it hit me. "You...you're talking about the stripper I hooked up with after my boy's bachelor party, right?"

"I don't know who she was, but I do remember that you played the heck out of me that night. It disturbed me so bad. I liked you a lot, Jaylin, and there were so many things that you had said and done to me that truly hurt my feelings."

I eased my hands away from hers and sat back in the chair. I never intentionally did things to hurt women's feelings, but it happened that way sometimes. I swallowed the lump in my throat and tried to explain my actions as best as I could.

"Check this out. I was young and going through some personal things at that time. I guess you wanted more than I was willing to offer, and I wasn't prepared to settle down with no one. I don't understand why you still have regrets about us. It was a long time ago and we both have moved on."

She sighed and started to nibble on her fingernails. "We have moved on, but I wanted to apologize to you for giving you gonor-rhea. I figured that's why you had been upset with me and it had been a while before I found out I had it. I had been seeing this other dude too, but when I stopped by your house that night, I wanted to tell you that I was pregnant. I had no idea who fathered my child and I needed, so badly, to talk to you that night. I was confused. I thought about suicide and everything. You have no idea how miserable I was that day, and how you played me didn't help."

I edged up from my seat, already feeling the beads of sweat dotting my forehead. The gonorrhea thing hadn't shocked me. After all of this time, I thought the stripper had given it to me. But the news about her being pregnant left my mouth dry.

"You were pregnant and didn't say anything to me? If we couldn't talk that night, there were plenty of more opportunities to do it."

"I know. But I had a lot of stuff going on. I was embarrassed about giving you a STD, and I wasn't sure if the baby was yours or his."

My stomach tightened. I couldn't wait to ask what happened to the baby.

Brashaney squeezed her forehead and swallowed. "I aborted the baby. I guess God is punishing me now, because I haven't been able to conceive another child since then. That's why I have so many regrets. I felt a need to tell you how sorry I was for what I did to you."

I wasn't sure how I felt right now. The 'what if the baby was mine' kept rushing to my thoughts, and relief was there as well. I had made some horrible mistakes with women, but my only regrets revolved around Nokea.

"Let's just say that I forgive you, only if you can forgive me for the way I acted," I said. "I'm well aware that I was a piece of work, and you were pretty brave for hanging in there with me. As far as the baby is concerned, I hate that you took that route, but I know that you had to do what was best for you. I hope that you'll be able to conceive again. In due time, I'm sure that you will."

Unlike earlier, this time around, Brashaney looked relieved. She stood with a huge smile on her face, and opened her arms for another hug.

"Stay sweet for me," I said as we embraced. "I hope you feel better and thanks for stopping by to get that off your chest."

"No, thank you for being so understanding. You're a good man, Jaylin. I hope you know that."

"Sometimes," I said, as we let go of each other. We walked to the door, where I opened it up and told her to be careful on the drive home.

"I will. Take care."

Brashaney checked out of Hell House on a good note. Right after she left, Jada and Chase popped out from behind the wall and couldn't wait to grill me.

"I done burnt plenty of niccas in my lifetime," Jada said, laughing. "But I'll be damned if I 'fess up and tell them about it. She was a brave bitch. And then to turn around and tell you about the abortion? Some hoes don't know when to quit."

"You gotta give her credit for being honest," Chase said. "At least she told him."

"Really? Is that what you call bein' honest? Showin' up years later—Jaylin, how many years has it been?"

"It's been a long time, but none of that matters anymore. She got the closure she needed and that's what's up. For now, I'm feeling up to a pillow fight or some pillow talk tonight. Whatever y'all down for, I'm gaming."

"Both," Chase said, running off to the bedroom. She was giddy as ever. Sexy as ever, too. I couldn't help but to wonder if she would someway or somehow fit into my circle. It was just a thought.

The pillow fight left me with a headache, but all of us were still hyped. We went to the game room to hang out. Roc and Jada started shooting pool, while Chase and I hooked ourselves up at the bar.

"What can I serve you?" Chase asked from behind the bar. She was dressed in a soft blue negligee that hid the good stuff. I had on a burgundy robe, and Sperry house shoes covered my feet. Roc was in his pajama pants, and Jada was in her cotton pajamas with elephant house shoes.

"If you've been paying attention to me like I think you have, then you already know what you can serve me."

Chase didn't hesitate. "Remy, no ice. Stay right there. I got you."

While Chase made our drinks, I turned on the swivel stool to watch Jada and Roc shoot pool. Jada was already fussing.

"The only balls I know about are the ones I occasionally put in my mouth. Now, tell me, again. What am I supposed to do with these hard balls on the table?"

Roc was in position to take his shot, so he did. "I can't believe you've never played pool before. Where in the hell have you been?"

"At ya Mama's house washin' yo dirty clothes. I didn't say that I haven't played before. What I'm sayin' is I don't know how. Y'all act like I'm supposed to know how to do all of this stuff, but some people ain't no sports fantastic like y'all are."

I stared at Jada, shaking my head. She had to be bullshitting with us. I found it hard to believe that her vocabulary was that fucked up. Roc got to her before I did.

"You don't have to be a sports *fanatic* to know how to shoot pool. And what the fuck is a sports fantastic? You know you be trippin,' ma."

Jada put her hands on her hip and her neck started to roll. She tore into Roc about correcting her and even put the pool stick up to his face, daring him to correct her again.

"Jaylin, you'd better come get this fool before I hurt him. All I'm tryin' to do is learn how to play pool, not be given an English lesson by somebody who ain't got no crudentals to teach me."

"Leave me out of it,' I said. "But just so you know, the word is *credentials*, baby. I'm just saying, so don't get all flustered with me for telling you. You need to listen to that man. I'm sure he's capable of helping you with the game as well as with your language."

Roc laughed, but Jada playfully pushed his shoulder. "Ain't nothin' funny, Roc. You know doggone well that yo language ain't intact either. I've heard you say some shit that left me scratchin' my head, but you didn't hear me say nothin'."

Roc defended himself. "Like what? Tell me what I've said that you didn't understand."

"I'll think of somethin'. But in the meantime, do you like grapes?"

"Grapes? Why?"

"I want to know because I had a dream that you and Jaylin were feedin' me some grapes."

"Naw, I don't like grapes. And I definitely wouldn't have fed them to you in a dream. Maybe somethin' else, but fasho not no grapes."

Jada rolled her eyes. "Now, why doesn't that surprise me? You were mean to me in that dream, but Jaylin was real nice." Jada looked over at me. "You like grapes, don't you?"

"Love them, especially with a tuna sandwich."

Jada's eyes widened. She had a startled look on her face. "Sandwich? Did you say sandwich?"

"Yes, did I say it incorrectly? What's the big deal?"

"I'm not gon' even say, but there was definitely a sandwich in my dream too. How did you know that it was? Did you have the same dream?"

"No. But I am a mind reader. I predict that if you don't stop playing around and get back to shooting pool, Roc gon' get real pissed."

"Too bad. He called me a chunky chick in my dream anyways, so I'm mad at him."

"I wouldn't even get at you like that, ma, so forget about the dream and handle yo business on this pool table."

While Jada and Roc continued their game, I turned around on the stool. Chase had just dropped a cherry into her drink that looked to be mixed with several different alcohols. She placed my drink in front of me and lifted her glass.

"Let's toast to may the best person win this Hell House challenge. I'm sure it'll be me, but you're entitled to keep hoping," she said.

I picked up my drink, but skipped the toast. I washed the Remy down in two swallows, then put the glass back on the bar.

"I would ask for a refill, but I prefer not to get too fucked up tonight. My mind doesn't always function right when alcohol consumes me."

Chase picked up the bottle of Remy, pouring me another glass.

"I say drink up. You only live once, and usually, people do what they really want to do, with or without alcohol. I hear that alcohol is an excuse for those who like to be naughty. What say you?"

"I say one more drink should put me in the mood and let me know where I want to venture to tonight. Right now, I have no idea, but I'm sure I'll know something soon."

I tossed another shot back and watched Chase down another drink. Unfortunately, I had a hard time getting with her. She reminded me too much of my son's mother, Scorpio. She used her good pussy to fuck with my head. I didn't like that shit. I always had to be in control, and I felt weak when I wasn't. So, in a nutshell, I didn't give a care how many drinks Chase poured. Nothing was going down with us tonight. Sex between us would only happen if or when I wanted it to, and as of yet, I wasn't ready to make that move.

"So," Chase said, looking at my empty glass. "What are you thinking?"

"I'm thinking that I'm going to call it a night."

"Good. I'm thinking the same thing. Do you mind if I cuddle in bed with you? I'll keep my hands to myself, only because I have other things on my mind and sex isn't one of them."

I guess she thought I was going to elaborate or push, but I didn't. We made our way to the bedroom together, feeling slightly tipsy. I held Chase close to me in bed, and as she rubbed my chest, I planted a soft kiss on her forehead. I suspected that she saw my dick rise through my jockey shorts, but that was because one head was thinking before the other one was allowed to do it. Chase rubbed her soft legs against mine, and then she started to suck on my neck. *So much for sex not being on her mind*, I thought.

"Anybody ever tell you that you're overly aggressive, and being that way can be a turnoff for some men?"

Chase halted her sucks on my neck and lowered her hand from my chest to my steel.

"How many times do you have to say it? You're a smart man, Jaylin, so put your right head to good use. Did you ever think that there may be a motive behind my actions? After all, this is a challenge, isn't it? And, if you're so turned off, I can't tell. Your dick is swelled to capacity. You must be aiming to put it somewhere. Somewhere wet and warm, I hope."

"Wet and warm, I welcome. But that would mean your mouth, and not your pussy. I'm not ready to tamper with that yet, so slide down, open wide, and please don't bite me."

Chase lowered herself underneath the covers and attempted to break me down with her skillful head job that made my eyes flutter. I couldn't deny that I was ready to slip my dick into her, but timing was everything. She wasn't the only one who had a motive. I did too, but I considered it more of a master plan that no one would see coming.

Roc

The one thing that I appreciated about this house was the work-out room. I got it in almost every day and so did Jaylin. The ladies came in from time to time, like this morning when Chase was on the elliptical machine and Jada was on the bike with a Pop-Tart dangling from her mouth. I was lifting weights while Jaylin was running on the treadmill. We all were watching TV and we stopped when we saw Jeff enter the room. Seeing him always meant some-thing was about to go down. I sat up on the bench, giving him my attention.

"Good morning," he said to all of us.

Everybody spoke back.

He put his foot on one of the weight benches, and like always, raked his fingers through his hair.

"I have good news today and bad news. The good news is that you'll get a chance to reach out to your family members or friends today. That bad news is that only one of you will be able to do it. I know how anxious you all have been to reach out, but the person whose name I pull will be able to make two phone calls. You must use my cell phone to place the calls, and the only thing you can't do is tell the people you speak to the location of this house."

This was good news to me. I hadn't spoken to Desa Rae or my

kids in quite some time. Jaylin seemed anxious to reach out to his family and so did Jada. Chase, I wasn't so sure. She didn't talk about family much, but when we wrote our names on paper and gave them back to Jeff, she crossed her fingers, in hopes that her name would get pulled.

"Good luck," Jeff said, shaking up our names in a box. He asked Jada to pull a name. She gave the piece of paper back to Jeff and when he opened it he said, "Roc."

That was music to my ears. With disappointed looks on their faces, the others got back to their workout. Jeff gave me his cell phone.

"How much time I got?" I asked.

"No time limit, but please don't take long. Remember to only make two phone calls. If my phone happens to ring, let me know."

I walked off and made my way to the patio to take a seat in one of the lounging chairs. With it being Sunday, I suspected that Desa Rae was at home. I couldn't wait to speak to her, but I almost fucked up somebody when a man answered the phone. Thick wrinkles lined my forehead, as I yelled into the phone. "Who the fuck is this?"

"Who the hell is this?"

"Nigga, this Roc. Where in the hell is Desa Rae?"

Whoever the fool was, he must have put the phone down. Soon after, Desa Rae responded. "Hello. Who is this?"

"Who the fuck was that answerin' yo phone?"

"That was Reggie, Roc. Latrel and Angelique stopped by and he came over."

"That's fine and dandy, but he still ain't got no business answerin' yo phone. Then, that nigga ain't never there when I'm there. Why all of a sudden he's there when I'm away?"

I could hear Desa Rae sigh, but she owed me a goddamn explanation. "I was getting Chassidy something to eat, and when the phone rang, I asked Reggie to reach over and get it. I'm not delighted about him being here either, Roc, but for the sake of Latrel's limited visit, I thought it would be a good idea if his father came here."

"I don't like your idea and yo ass gon' be in real big trouble when I get there."

"I hope so because I miss you so very much. How's everything going?"

Hearing her say that she missed me calmed me down a bit. Besides, it felt good to hear her voice. "It's a'ight. The house is cool, but I'm ready to get this shit over with. I got a good chance at winnin' this thing. I'm glad you suggested that I come here to get away for a while. I know you got tired of me bein' there all the time, but I can't help myself."

"I never get tired of you being here. I want to make sure you're doing things that don't always include me, and I know you needed a break from the shop. I'm happy about the amount of time that we spend together, so don't you go thinking that I'm not."

"I feel ya, ma. But you'd better get used to me being around all the time, especially when I officially become your husband. You still got on my ring, don't you?"

"Of course I do. What would make you think that I've taken it off?"

"I'on know. You got that nigga back there laughin' and shit like everything all good between y'all. I hear him in the background talkin'. You know that him bein' there is makin' me real uncomfortable."

"I'm surprised to hear you say that. My question to you is do you trust me? Have I ever given you a reason not to?"

I thought about how Desa Rae had been on the up-and-up since

I'd known her. It was me who had slipped and bumped my head a few times, not her. "Yeah, ma, you know I trust you. I just wish I was there with you, that's all."

"Well, there is nothing that says you have to stay there. You can leave on your own free will, right?"

"I can, but I like to compete. You got me into this mess and it's kind of hard for me to walk away from it. I suspect that it won't go on for three months because we've already lost two people. It's been some crazy shit goin' on. I can't wait to tell you all about it."

"Is that right?" she said, laughing. "I can't wait to hear about it. Meanwhile, your daughter is pulling on this phone, eager to speak to you. Hold on, okay?"

Desa Rae gave Chassidy the phone. It felt so good to hear her voice. She went on and on about what she'd been doing, and told me what Desa Rae had been up to as well. I couldn't help it that I was tuning into the background, where I could still hear Reggie laughing and having a slap-happy good time with my woman. I despised that nigga and everything about him. The last thing I remembered, Desa Rae told me that he was upset about her being pregnant by me. According to her, he wanted no part of Chassidy, so why in the fuck was he there? This shit didn't sit right with me, but I did my best to make the best of this conversation. Chassidy told me she loved me, and after I shot love back to her, Desa Rae spoke again.

"Chassidy's whole attitude has changed since you called," she said. "You should see this big-ole smile on her face. And if you get a chance, please contact Vanessa to see if her mother can bring Li'l Roc over. I don't mind going to pick him up, but she may have a problem with that."

"I only get two phone calls, so I'll call her next. Don't you have her mother's number?"

"I had it somewhere, but I can't find it. Either way, I'm sure they would rather speak to you than me."

Desa Rae told me to hold on. I heard her saying something in the background. She laughed and told Latrel to stop doing that. I was irritated. When she returned to the phone, she told me Latrel said hello.

"Tell him I said what's up. I'mma let you get back to your company, but I had to holla whenever the opportunity became available."

"I'm so glad that you called, because you've been on my mind a lot. I honestly didn't think I'd miss you this much, but I guess I should have known better."

"Same here. Maybe this is what we needed to realize how strong our love really is."

She had the audacity to say something to somebody in the background again. "I'm sorry, baby. What did you say?"

"Nothin' important. But, uh, look. I need to gone and get off this phone right now. I'll make sure Vanessa or her mother contacts you about Li'l Roc."

"You do that, okay? We're on our way to dinner, but I'll have my cell phone with me."

"Dinner? Is Reggie goin' too?"

Desa Rae paused for a few seconds. "Yes, I think so. Latrel asked him to come along."

I couldn't believe how swoll I was, but what the fuck could I do right now? "Enjoy your dinner. Kiss my baby for me, and I'll check in again when I can."

"I will. I love you, sweetheart. See you soon."

"Yeah, me too."

I ended the call with a bad taste in my mouth. Yeah, I trusted Desa Rae, but I damn sure didn't trust Reggie. I took a deep breath, then called Vanessa's cell phone to see what was up with Li'l Roc.

"I don't recognize this number, so speak fast before I hang up," she said.

"Roc. And you'd better not hang up on me."

She laughed. "Never. What's up, boo?"

"Where Li'l Roc at?"

"He's at my mama's house. Why don't you call over there to speak to him?"

"I can't. I only get two phone calls and I already used one."

"I guess I don't have to ask who you called first. I can't believe you're serious about marryin' that heifer, Desa Rae, and you already know how I feel about her. She's been nice to Li'l Roc, but I don't like how she talks to me when I call over there to speak to him."

"You know I don't appreciate you talkin' down on her like that, so watch yourself, all right? You doin' you these days, I'm doin' me, and nothin' else needs to be said."

"There's a lot that needs to be said, but how I feel don't matter. All I'm askin' for is a little respect from yo woman. I saw her at the grocery store last week and she didn't even speak to me. Maybe because there was a man helpin' her with her groceries and she didn't want me to see her."

I bit into my bottom lip, wondering if Vanessa was trying to fuck with my head. "You want respect, give it. Desa Rae has reached out to you plenty of times only to get slapped in her face. That's why she prefers to deal with yo mama. I don't know why she wouldn't speak to you at the grocery store, and that was probably a bagger helpin' her with those bags."

"I don't give a shit who he was. She should have spoken to me. And for him to be a bagger, she was awfully chummy with him. I guess I would've been too, 'cause he was fine as hell."

"I know what your idea of fine is. If he looked anything like that

muthafucka you datin', I can't take your word for it. Call your
mama and tell her to call Desa Rae so Li'l Roc can go over there
and spend some time with his sister. I'm gettin' ready to check
out of here, but tell my son I love him."

"What about me?"

"What about you?"

"Do you still love me?"

Without answering, I hung up, mad as hell. Vanessa called back,
and I had to quickly answer the phone so Jeff wouldn't hear it ring.

"This phone does not belong to me, so please do not use this
number again."

"That's cool, but you had no business hangin' up on me. All I
asked was a question. If you ain't man enough to answer it, then
don't."

"Here's your answer. No, I don't. Now are you satisfied?"

"I'm not, because I don't believe you. Anyways, I went to holla
at the fellas at your shop the other day. My car was leakin' some
oil and Romo fixed it for me. They talked about how much they
missed you around there, but them niggas were clownin.' You may
want to hurry home. There were a lot of unhappy customers gripin'
about how long they had to wait. You didn't get yo information
from me, but you know I always got yo back, right?"

"So you say. And thanks for the info. You know I appreciate it."

"You'd better."

I told Vanessa that I had to go. The news about my business had
me worried, so I glanced at the workout room to see what Jeff was
doing. He was still running his mouth, so I rushed to call Craig to
find out what was up.

"You've reached Roc's Place, and unfortunately, there is no sane
person here to take your call," Craig said in a proper voice, laughing.

"Naw, I'm just playin'. What up? This Craig. How can I help you?"

I didn't think a damn thing was funny. "Yeah, you can help me by gettin' yo shit together and stop playin' around. What's this I hear about some of my customers bein' angry because service is shitty?"

Craig cleared his throat. "What's up, Boss? I don't know where you got yo info from, but since you've been gone, I only had one customer complaint. You know how these people do it around here, and that chick was mad because she didn't want to pay what I told her she had to."

I looked up and could see Jeff coming my way. "I need to make this quick. When I get back, and it will be soon, there betta not be no bullshit goin' on. If there is, nobody will get paid, and I mean that shit. Tell my niggas I said what's up, and stop answerin' my phone like a damn idiot. Keep it professional, a'ight?"

"No problem, Boss. See you soon."

I ended the call and reached out to give Jeff his phone. "I had to make another call, pertain' to my business. It was urgent, and I hope there won't be no problem."

Jeff said everything was good. We stood around yakking for a while, then he left. I was swoll about my conversation with Desa Rae. Even though she didn't know it, she was damn sure on my shit list. So was Craig. I already knew there would be a lot of ass kickings to deliver whenever I got on my turf, and after those phone calls, I was anxious to get home and see what was really up.

Jada

Thanks to Prince leaving his blow behind, Roc was around here getting high as the sky. Then again, so was I. Every time I saw him hemmed up somewhere, I joined right in with him.

I guess I couldn't help myself. Being in this house was starting to work my nerves. Everybody had issues, and I was doing my best to watch my back. That was how I managed to see Chase creeping that night. She thought I had gone to bed, but I saw her go into the bathroom and change clothes. Then I saw her tiptoeing outside, so I followed her. When I saw her standing beside the workout room, I squinted and saw Jeff out there too. Something didn't add up to me. I wasn't up for no trickery shit between the two of them, and it was apparent that something fishy was going on.

The day after that one, I caught up with Chase outside, where I teased her about having jungle fever. Her eyes widened like saucers. She damn near choked, but I gave her a hint that I knew what was up.

Since then, she'd been extremely nice to me. She kept asking questions, trying to see if I was going to tell her what I saw. I planned on telling her, but not until I was ready.

After a few more hits from a joint, I was ready to confront Chase. Roc and I was in the closet laughing and acting silly. When I pushed him backward, he fell into one of the shelves, knocking it down.

"Damn, girl," he said, giggling. "Stop ruffin' me up. You don't need to smoke no more of dis' shit if it got you wantin' to throw punches."

"Stop bein' such a wimp and pick that shelf up. You got my stuff on the floor, and you know Jaylin gon' come in here clownin' when he see his stuff scattered."

"Buck that nigga. I'm not pickin' that shelf up, 'cause yo ass the one who made me do it."

"Hold that thought, baby. I'll be right back."

Roc laughed as I left the closet, knowing damn well that I wasn't coming back anytime soon. I left the bedroom and caught up with Chase as she was sitting at the kitchen table with Jaylin, putting together a puzzle.

"Hey, Jaylin," I said. "Roc said that he needed some help with a shelf in the closet that fell down. Go in there and help that brotha. Please."

"You look messed up, Jada," he said. "Y'all need to chill with smoking weed every day."

"Daddy, the bag is almost gone, so don't worry your fine li'l self about me. Just gon' in there and help Roc, before he breaks somethin' else."

Jaylin left the kitchen in a hurry. Probably because he didn't want nobody to damage his stuff. I sat at the table across from Chase and picked up a puzzle piece.

"This looks like a hard-ass puzzle to put together. How many pieces is it?"

"Twenty-five-hundred pieces. Jaylin seems to think that we can have this put together by the end of the day. But as you can see, that's not going to happen."

"I can bet you some money that it ain't goin' to happen. I will also bet you that you won't be the last person in this house, especially if I go tell Jaylin and Roc about what I saw the other night."

Chase's brows shot up. She swallowed and slowly laid her puzzle piece on the table. She then turned her head, looking toward the bedroom. "Wha…what did you exactly see the other night?"

"You know what I saw. Or do you prefer that I spell it out for you?"

"You're going to have to spell it out for me. I have no idea what you're talking about."

"Chase, don't play stupid with me. You cool and everything, but I hate for people to play me like I'm stupid. Why don't you go ahead and tell me what's really goin' on with you and Jeff? Is this some kind of game, and are you tryin' to set us up so that you'll win, no matter what? I need some answers or else I'mma blow this whole thing wide open."

Chase looked over her shoulder again at the bedroom door. She stood up from the table. "Come on and go outside with me. I don't want to talk in here."

I shook my head from side to side. "No, no ma'am. Unfortunately, I'm not goin' anywhere but right here. You may try to push me into the water and drown me, especially since I know what I know."

"I'm not a killer, nor am I here to hurt anyone. You need to lay off that weed. It has you very paranoid. Just trust me on this. Come outside for a few minutes. Please."

I hesitated, but then I got up from the table. If Chase tried some slick shit, I was going to knock her clean up side her head. Before I went outside with her, I snatched a broom from the closet and grabbed some chips to help with my munchies.

Chase laughed and threw her hand back at me.

"Bitch, I don't see nothin' funny. I really don't trust you, and I'mma always do what I got to do to protect myself."

She put her hand on her hip. "With a broom, Jada? What in the hell is a broom supposed to do?"

We went outside and sat close by the door. "You must ain't never been a disobedient child growin' up. 'Cause if you were, you would know exactly how much damage a broom can do. Don't underestimate the power of it."

"Okay, I won't, especially since you got a tight grip on it. When it comes to being a disobedient child, trust me when I say I was one. I had every reason to be one, because my mother betrayed me and my father sexually abused me. I hated the both of them, but that was then and this is now."

"I'm sorry to hear that, but what does that have to do with what's goin' on right now?"

"Not much. Then again, I just learned that there may be something very fascinating about my past that's going to help me win this challenge."

There was something real wicked in Chase's eyes. Almost scary, in a sense, so I had to see what was up. "We already know that you ain't got it all upstairs, Chase, but you need to seriously let go of the bitterness inside of you. I don't really care about your troubles as a kid. I came out here to find out what was up with you and that white boy."

Chase appeared irritated by my comment. She crossed her legs and clamped her hands together. "Okay, Jada. I was going to spill the truth to you at a later date, but since you're forcing this out of me now, I guess I have no choice but to spill the beans. But please understand that I can't tell you everything right now, because I need to get the facts. Some secrets have to wait until later."

"Girl, you are startin' to work my nerves. Would you please get to the point?"

Chase paused, then released a deep sigh. "I found a way to get Jaylin and Roc out of this house. In order for me to do it, I had to get to know more about their personal lives and backgrounds. So what I did was I started to make a connection with Jeff through email. I flirted with him and told him I was interested in us hooking up. He fell for it. On three occasions, he came to see me while everyone was asleep. During his visits, yes, sometimes we had sex, but I also asked him for information about Roc and Jaylin. Jeff gave it to me. Just by having their personal information, I'm in a position to share some things with their loved ones that may cause harm. I'm hoping that the information that I share will send them packing."

"Oooo, you are so darn sneaky. But if you got information on them, I know you got some stuff on me."

"Just a little stuff, but none of that matters."

My jaw dropped. I couldn't believe that she had found out some stuff about me. "If it don't matter to you, it surely matters to me. Tell me what you found out or else I start talkin' right now."

Chase exhaled. "Okay, Jada. I said none of this matters, but I do know that you were locked up for thirty days for shoplifting. I also know that you have several assault charges on your police record and that you live in a Section 8 apartment complex. You don't have a great relationship with your mother, father abandoned you, and you don't have any children. Your husband has a long criminal record, but it appears that many of the other men you've dated have criminal records too. You haven't had a stable job since the 90s, and you currently have a warrant out for your arrest for two unpaid traffic tickets. You didn't graduate from high school and when you lived in Los Angeles—"

"Okay, stop right there," I said with my mouth hanging wide open. I couldn't even express how I felt, but I was damn sure mad about this bitch digging into my background. There was no doubt that she was right on the money. "I didn't hear you mention my social security number, blood type, or what size drawers I wear. You also didn't mention how many times I go to the library or what grocery store I normally shop at. You have violated my privacy. I'm gon' have to check the hell out of you and Jeff for oversteppin' y'all's bounties."

"Jada, please listen to what I'm saying to you. The word is *boundaries*, not bounties. But none of that matters. When we win this challenge, you can take the money to clear those warrants. You can move out of your Section 8 apartment and go live happily ever after. We've all got ugly things in our past, but this is about your future. Don't blow it, okay?"

I thought about what she'd said. Maybe I was overreacting. "Just so you know, that Section 8 apartment costs me $225 a month and my friend's name is on it, not mine. And those traffic tickets were because I let a no-good fool use my car. He was the one who got those tickets. We all shoplift from time to time, but I happened to get caught up that day. And as for my associates' criminal records, that's on them, not me."

"Thanks for telling me, but I don't care. What I care about is winning this thing so we can have some money."

"Let's be real here. A hundred thousand, divided by two, that ain't really what I consider my ticket out of the ghetto. It will help, though, but what exactly do you need me to do? Just so you know, I'm not fuckin' nobody unless I want to. And I'm not killin' nobody either."

"I'm not asking you to do anything of the such. All I may need, right now, is for you to get some explicit pictures for me. Good pictures of me and Roc, and of me and Jaylin. I'm going to start turning up the heat on both of them. I need for you to catch the action."

"This startin' to sound like some Inspector Gadget or James Bond bullshit. How am I supposed to get photos when we don't have cameras, phones, or nothin'?"

"Oh, yes, we do. Jeff provided those things for me, but you can't let Jaylin or Roc see them. I really need to know that I can trust you on this, Jada. I can't afford to have none of that backstabbing mess that Sylvia was doing going on. If you truly want this money, all I'm saying is that I can hand half of it over to you on a silver platter, guaranteed. All you have to do is follow my lead."

Chase looked over my shoulder and whispered that Jaylin and Roc were coming.

"We'll continue our talk later," she whispered.

I nodded and couldn't help but to think more about the money. I could almost taste it. If she had a way to make us winners, I was all for it. Plus, I would get the money that Jaylin had promised me. I wasn't going to tell Chase about that money. It was none of her business. She seemed to have this all planned out. Either she was clever or awfully stupid, especially with trusting Jeff to stay quiet. I was going with the flow, in hopes that trusting her wouldn't get me tossed out of Hell House on my ass.

Now that the cat was out of the bag, I had some serious planning to do. I felt as if Jada would have my back; after all, it was all about the money for her. For me, it was about that too, but it was also about being able to leave this house with my head held up high. I wasn't going out like Pooky and them. Or should I say like Sylvia, who left here dissed. No way would I let the men have that kind of bragging rights.

For the next several days, I did everything in my power to get closer to Roc and Jaylin. After my oral performance the other night, Jaylin had been riding me too. I must say that the feel of his dick in my mouth felt good. I thoroughly enjoyed the taste of his semen, but it was time for me to get mine too.

Until then, I cooked healthy meals for Jaylin and made sure the house was spotless. Roc didn't have many gripes, but when he complained about his back one night, I massaged it for him. They were always looking for competitive things to do, so I apologized to Roc for my lack of effort on the tennis court and teamed up with him during another game of volleyball in the pool. Needless to say, we won. I played video games with them, and Jaylin and I finished the puzzle.

There was no doubt that the house had become drama free, even though Jada had something smart to say every once in a while. Roc seemed more relaxed, but more than anything, I think the weed he'd been smoking was helping him cope with what was bugging him. Jaylin's source of comfort for whatever he was dealing with was alcohol and conversation. I noticed him picking up the bottle more often, but I guess everybody had their way of coping with being here.

As for me, I didn't need any source of drugs or alcohol to get me through. That kind of stuff made people lose focus and take their eyes off the prize. So while all of them had been getting it in with their drugs and alcohol, I was watching and paying attention. I eavesdropped on a conversation that I heard Jaylin and Roc having while in the workout room. Jaylin was holding the punching bag for Roc while he let out his frustrations. They didn't know I was right outside the door, but it was apparent that Roc had some trust issues with Desa Rae.

"I don't like the way this shit got me feelin'," Roc grunted while punching the bag. "I find it odd that the nigga hadn't shown up once while I was there. Now all of a sudden, he over there lolly gaggin' with Desa Rae. Somethin' don't add up for me."

"You're going back and forth. One minute, you say you trust her. The next minute, you're saying something else. In order for you to be at ease about the situation, you gotta go with what you firmly believe. Do you honestly believe that she over there fucking her ex-husband?"

Roc hesitated to answer, then punched the bag again. "On a for real tip, I don't know what to believe. I have a hard time trusting women, only because I know how sneaky their asses can be. They'll have you believin' things are all good, and then you find out another story when the next brotha shows up."

"I must say that I agree with you on that. I stopped trusting women a long time ago. There were way too many of them playing games and keeping secrets. That's what gets me. They are so good at keeping secrets. You can lay your shit on the line and they'll still keep those skeletons locked up in the closet. So, I definitely understand how you're feeling about Desa Rae. If you're that concerned about the situation at home, why don't you wrap this up and check out of here?"

Roc stopped punching the bag and took deep breaths. "You couldn't be serious. Leave so you can jet with the cash and braggin' rights? It ain't goin' down like that, so my issues with Desa Rae will be left for another day. When all is said and done, I'm goin' to be the last person in this house."

Jaylin didn't respond. He squinted while looking at the door. I suspected that he saw me. I quickly widened the door as if I hadn't been standing there all along.

"Hello, fellas," I said, making my way over to the elliptical machine.

They spoke. Lust filled their eyes, as I put in a little something extra today to get their attention. My hair was in a sleek ponytail, showing the true beauty of my makeup-free face.

The spandex that I wore was all black. It hugged every curve in my well-defined body. The zipper in the front stopped right at my firm breasts that sat up high. My ass appeared more plump than usual, and the way they stared at me, I knew it looked good. I had on no panties whatsoever. The spandex slipped right between my coochie lips, showing a lip-licking camel toe that I was sure they appreciated.

Before I got on the elliptical machine, I stretched on a floor mat, showing how flexible I was. I noticed Jaylin and Roc taking peeks at me and then at each other. When I bent over to touch my toes, I heard Roc clear his throat. I then lifted my leg ballerina style, and that was when I caught Jaylin licking his lips. This was very much turning out as I had planned.

I was done stretching, so I stepped on the elliptical machine and got to work. The one thing that I knew for a fact was that men loved to see, and or watch, a woman sweat. I also knew that when you backed off from showing them attention, they'd surely give it to you in return.

I put the machine on the highest level, and within five to ten minutes, sweat started to trickle down my body. The faster I went, the more I sweated. The more I sweated, the louder my grunts became.

"Uhhh, umm, ahhh." I sounded as if I were having an orgasm.

"Don't hurt yourself over there, baby," Jaylin advised.

"Right. Damn sure sounds like you gettin' it in, ma."

"A girl's gotta do what she must to stay in shape," I said. "Especially when she's preparing herself to get into shape for all of the right reasons."

They didn't dare touch that comment, so I kept it moving. I didn't even stop when Jada came into the room complaining.

"Bitch, you makin' me look real bad," she shouted to me. "I may as well get the hell out of here before I embarrass myself."

Jada headed for the door, but Roc and Jaylin teased her, encouraging her to stay.

"Don't be walking out of here because Chase looking sexier than a mutha on that elliptical," Jaylin said. "Even though you can't pull that off, you still need to stay and try something."

Roc laughed and cosigned. "Right, ma, stay. But don't get on the treadmill today. Please. Why not lift some weights instead?"

Jada slapped her leg and fake laughed with them. "Hee-haw. I see you fools got jokes today, right? We'll soon see who gon' have the last laugh. All I can say is it won't be you two crooked-dick niggas."

Jada rolled her eyes. She looked real upset when she left, but they shrugged it off.

"That's the second time she's gone there with that crooked dick shit." Jaylin shook his head. "What in the hell is she talking about?"

"Don't know, don't care. As long as my shit is, it bends a little bit, but only when it has to curve into somethin'."

Jaylin slapped his hand against Roc's. They got back to working out.

Nearly an hour later, I finished up and wiped down my face with a fluffy white towel. I was breathing hard, so I bent over to get some water from the fountain. Saying nothing else, I headed for the door.

"Chase," Jaylin called out to me. I turned around to see what he wanted. He winked. "Looking good, baby. Keep up the good work."

I nodded and heard Roc say "umph" as I walked out the door. *Got'em*, I thought. This was the turning point I had hoped for.

After leaving the workout room, I headed for the bedroom to gather clean clothes and take a shower. Outside of the bedroom door, I could hear Jada speaking to someone. Since I had given her one of the cell phones Jeff gave me, I hurried to open the door. Sure enough, she was sitting on the bed laughing and talking to someone.

"What are you doing?" I shouted.

"Girl, let me call you back. Okay," she said, laughing again before ending the call. She put the phone beside her and shot me an evil stare.

"What was that all about?" I asked. "I told you to be careful about that phone, Jada. Are you trying to get us busted or what?"

"I haven't spoken to my girl in a while, so I figured I'd give her a quick call. Regardless, you don't have to shout at me like I'm some little kid or somethin', do you?"

Yes, this bitch was working my nerves, but the truth of the matter was I needed her in order to pull this off. I needed for her to fall in line so we could hurry up and get this over with. "I apologize for raising my voice, but come on, Jada. I thought I could trust you. What if Roc or Jaylin would've walked in here and saw you with that cell phone? All they had to do was tell Jeff and he'd be walking you out of here."

"I thought you had the hook up with Jeff? If you do, then you should be able to make sure I stay in this house, no matter what I do."

My face fell flat. No she wasn't trying to go there, especially when I was the one giving up the coochie to keep Jeff on my team. "That sounds like you're taking advantage of the situation. I'm sure Jeff is going to question me about you being on the phone. It's going to put me in a bad position. Just do both of us a huge favor and stay off the phone. This is almost over with. I don't want you doing anything to mess up our money."

Jada stood and stretched. "Sure, Chase. I won't call my friend again, but you gon' need to hurry this up, because I'm gettin' a li'l frustrated with Jaylin and Roc. They always sayin' stupid stuff. I don't think they realize how much that stuff hurts."

"Don't go getting all sensitive on me, and to hell with both of them. Who cares what they say? I'm going to need for you to come through for us. You'll feel so much better in another day or two. You can trust me on that."

"I hope so."

Jada walked toward the door. She smiled, making me feel a little bit better than I did after I came into the room. I grabbed several pieces of clothing from the closet and headed for the bathroom. Before showering, I leaned against the counter to call Jeff.

"Hey, beautiful," he said. "What's cooking?"

"Nothing much. I'm sure you saw Jada using the phone. I told her to knock it off before she got caught. She's very hardheaded, but I know for a fact that she wants this money more than I do."

"I hope she listens to you. I've seen her on the phone more than once. Roc almost caught her earlier, but she walked away and went outside. I don't know if it was a good idea for you to involve her."

I bit my nail, feeling the same way. "I'm with you on this, but I don't have a choice. She knows what's up with us, and I had to let her in on this so she wouldn't say anything. It's a done deal now, so I have to go with the flow."

"You don't have to do anything. Are you sure you don't want her kicked out of the house? She could be kicked out for breaking the rules, you know?"

"Yeah, but then Jaylin and Roc will question where she got the phone. I'm sure she'll tell them and point the finger at me. That wouldn't be smart on our part, so let it ride for now. Besides, Jaylin is already hanging on by a thread and he doesn't even know it. I guess you'll be paying him a visit real soon."

"Yes, soon. He is so done. As for you, my dear, you have me craving for you again."

I rolled my eyes, glad that he couldn't see me. The one thing I hated was clingy men who didn't know when they were being used. "Like I told Jada, we're getting so close to ending this. I don't want any fuck ups, especially since I noticed Jaylin and Roc paying more attention to me. Once this is done, you can have me when, where, or however you want me. Let's work on crossing the finish line first."

"Sounds good, babe. I'll see you soon."

"Great. And do me a small favor."

"What's that?"

"Bring me some Viagra. I may need it to speed things along."

Jeff laughed. "I will, sweetheart. But please don't hurt yourself."

I couldn't help but to laugh. "Never."

Wasting a little time before my shower, I went to the computer desk to check my fan mail. I had a lot of women griping about some of the things that I'd done, but their comments didn't bother me not one bit. They hadn't seen anything yet. This time, I intended to go all out.

The men who emailed me always wanted more. I read two emails from a man named Jerrod, and I brightened his day with a freaky response. Then I read an email from Laurel who didn't inform me where she lived.

Chase, I want to know why you think it is okay for you to date married men? That's my only issue with you. I sort of like your style because you remind me of myself, minus the married men thingy. If a man is married, you must know that he's off limits.

I rolled my eyes, but still replied to her email.

Laurel, the man has to determine if he's off limits, not me. It's not that I go around seeking married men, and truthfully, I prefer not to go there with them. But if one of them happens to make himself available to me, and I'm attracted to him, then I go for it. My demands are minimal, and I'm never interested in him separating from his wife. Nine times out of ten, that won't happen anyway, and I'm not one of those foolish mistresses who believe that it will. What I offer any man that I date is in-the-meantime, and in-between-time companionship. My time with men can be seen as therapeutic, and I'm being honest when I say that many of them really need my help. I don't know why people always see what I do as a negative thing, but my advice to married women would be to take good care of their husbands so women like me won't have to. The truth is sometimes hard to swallow, but I'm just keeping it real. If you've gotten to know me, you already know that's what I do. Gotta go, and I hope you continue to like my style.

I logged off the computer and returned to the bathroom to take my shower.

Jaylin

Something didn't feel right to me. I wasn't sure what it was, but it wasn't like me to feel paranoid for no particular reason. I guess the main reason that I had been feeling this way was because everybody left in the house was getting along too well. With women around, there was always a little attitude to be expected, but it was nowhere near to the level that it had been before. Even Roc and I were doing okay. I was starting to have much respect for him, and I understood where he was coming from about not trusting his woman. She had him somewhat tripping. He was high as hell almost every hour on the hour. If I was that upset, I seriously think I'd be at home by now, getting things in order.

I guess it showed me how serious he was about this challenge. But maybe not serious enough, since he hadn't been trying to get Chase out of here like he said he would. I was doing my best not to sweat him about it—considering what he was dealing with—but whenever I felt as though somebody was failing me, I had to pick up the pieces and handle things for myself. And as delightful as Chase had been looking these past few weeks, and after the way she waxed my dick, I was starting to feel as though picking up the pieces wouldn't be such a bad thing after all. Then again, maybe it was just me wanting to sample some new pussy.

My workout was done, so I wanted to shower. Somebody was already in the bathroom. I figured it was Chase, because Roc had gone for a swim and Jada was sitting on the couch pouting while watching TV. I assumed she was still upset about how our conversation went down earlier.

"Why your mouth still stuck out?" I asked, then took a seat, dressed in my gray sweatpants. A towel was in my hand, so I used it to wipe sweat from my face and bare chest.

"Don't say nothin' to me, Jaylin, especially if you don't have anything nice to say."

"I have said nice things to you, so I'm not sure what you're talking about."

"You know good and well what I'm talkin' about. How you gon' tell me I can't look sexy workin' out, so don't bother? I didn't think a woman had to look sexy workin' out, and too damn bad if I don't."

"I said you wouldn't look as sexy as Chase. Not that you wasn't sexy at all."

She folded her arms and pursed her lips even more. "So, in other words, you think I'm sexy, but not as sexy as Chase? Is that what you're sayin'?"

"What I'm saying is it doesn't matter what I think. What matters is what you believe about yourself."

"I get all of that, and you can trust and believe that I know I'm sexy, no matter what you say."

"Good, then why are you still pouting? It's like you saying my dick is crooked when I know it ain't."

"Well, maybe you should get a better look at that thing because it is crooked. Big time."

"No, it's not."

"Yes, it is."

"Do you want me to pull it out and show you that it's not crooked?"

"You can do whatever you want to, but I already saw how crooked it is."

I stood and dropped my sweats to my ankles. I stood nearly butt naked, causing her to jump back and move several inches away from me.

"Maybe you need to focus your eyes a little better or get some glasses." I looked down at my goods. "Where do you see a crooked dick?"

Jada sat up straight. She looked at my front side, then examined my back side. "It ain't hard yet. Wait until it gets hard, then I can show you how crooked it is."

I sat back on the couch, resting my arms on top of it. "Well, let's wait until it gets hard then."

Jada had a smirk on her face, trying not to laugh. "You don't have no shame in your game, do you? First, you put all that…that nail-grippin' ass in my face, and then you got this thing just layin' there like it ain't nothin'. You must think I'm a dyke or somethin', or that I'm in no way interested in men. Well, breakin' news, sweetheart. I will tear up somethin' like that. If you do not cover up that thing, my mouth is gon' make a crash landin' in your lap that may be very painful for you because I won't let up."

"See, you're not being fair. Don't hurt me. All I want to do is prove my point. Talk like that gon' keep it down, when I'm trying to get it to go up."

Jada cleared mucus from her throat and crossed her legs. "Aww, okay. So you need a li'l dirty talk, huh? Close your eyes and I'll whisper in your ear whatever comes to mind."

There was no way in hell Jada could get me hard, so I closed my eyes to fuck with her. She threw her heavy leg across my lap and leaned into my ear.

"Are you listenin'?" she whispered, then blew her hot breath on my ear.

I nodded.

"Good. Now relax and travel with me to Jaylin's land. A place where so many hoes done been, but the door remains open to plenty mo'. A place where coochies get wet, and you're willin' and able to satisfy them all. Yo crooked dick can make a woman holla at the top of her lungs, and—"

"I'm still not hard, and that mess you're talking is corny. Get to the point, or should I say, get to the good stuff."

Jada pushed my shoulder. "Just wait a minute, would you? I'm gettin' there." She cleared her throat again, then continued on. "It was the night before Christmas when we had passionate sex all through the house. Everybody was staring, even the mouse who couldn't believe how I straddled my big ass across yo lap and rode you until yo nuts fell off and—"

My eyes shot open. "This ain't working for me. You're heading in the wrong direction."

Jada snapped. "Patience. I said I'm gettin' there, so close your eyes. Please."

I closed my eyes, then cocked my neck from side to side. "Hurry up with this. I don't have all day."

"Yes you do. 'Cause ain't shit else to do around here but this. Now, where was I?"

"You were talking about cutting off my nuts."

"No, stupid, they fell off. But I caught them in my mouth before they hit the floor. And then, uh, what's one of your hoochies' names?"

"I don't do hoochies."

"Well, one of those cute, church-goin' girls who loves you. What's her name?"

"Nokea."

"No who?"

"No. Key. A."

"That's a fucked up name. What the heck was wrong with her parents, naming her after a phone? They on crack or what? Anyway, I caught yo nuts and Nokea swallowed yo dick."

I nodded. "You're on the right path. Stay that course and keep including Nokea."

I felt a smack on the back of my head and I opened my eyes.

"See, there you go insultin' me again," Jada griped. "I was tryin' to be nice to you, Jaylin, and I even included one of yo bitches. But you took my kindness and ran with it."

"Don't use that kind of language when you're referring to her, all right? You asked for a name and I gave you one. Don't be mad at me because you have no clue whatsoever what it means to talk dirty."

Jada cocked her head back. "What? I was—"

"What's going on in here?" Chase asked from behind us.

We turned around, only to see her with a towel wrapped around her naked body. My thoughts turned naughty. I visualized what was underneath the towel. Thought about her legs wrapped around my back while I rocked her pussy to sleep. I could feel my manhood rise to the occasion.

"I'll be damned," Jada said in awe as she looked down at my goods. "It's a miracle, and it doesn't take much, does it?"

Chase rolled her eyes and walked off. Any other time, she would have joined in, but not today. I held my meat in my hand, gripping it up.

"Now, show me where my dick is crooked."

"Let it go so it can stand up by itself."

I let it go and watched Jada examine it with bugged eyes. "It's uh, thick," she confirmed.

"Yes."

"Veeery long."

"Correct."

"Smooth."

"No doubt."

"Mouthwaterin'."

"Of course."

"Suckable."

"I would hope so."

"Satisfyin'."

"Always."

"Circumcised."

"Since day one."

"But I can honestly say that it's not crooked."

"No. Now where is my apology?"

"It's right between my legs. Would you like for me to give it to you now or later?"

"Nah, later. After I take a shower."

I stood and pulled up my sweats. When I looked up, to my surprise, Jeff was standing near the hallway.

"Sorry," he said, looking at me and Jada. "Did I interrupt something?"

"Hell, yes," Jada said. "I was gettin' ready to apologize to this man for all of the hurtful and wrong things that I've done and said about him. I need for him to accept my apology real soon. You interrupted my plea for him to forgive me to the fullest."

"I thought I heard him say that he forgave you," Jeff said, looking at me. "Didn't you?"

"I told her I would accept her apology later, but I think she may have wanted to give me a little something now."

"You two can work that out later. Right now, Jaylin, I need to speak to you about some concerns that I have."

I shrugged. "Sure. What's up?"

Jeff looked at Jada, who was all ears. She picked up a magazine and flipped through it, as if she was interested.

"Follow me." Jeff made his way toward the front of the house. I followed, wanting to find out what was on his mind.

He turned at the foyer to face me. "I need to be clear about something. There was a rule in this house about letting outsiders come in. You weren't supposed to do that, but the cameras caught you letting a woman inside."

At first, I didn't know what the hell Jeff was talking about, but then it hit me. "I assume you're talking about the maid, Brashaney. If you saw me on camera letting her inside, then there shouldn't be any questions asked. Her main purpose was to come here and clean this house. I got your permission to do that and you gave me clearance, didn't you?"

"Yes, I did. But she came back later that night. Roc opened the door, but he didn't allow her to come inside. You, however, did."

Jeff was starting to piss me off. It was like he was grasping at straws, trying to get me caught up. "I let her in here, but the only reason she was here to begin with was because she came to clean the house."

"That's not the only reason she was here. The bottom line is she shouldn't have been invited to come back inside, especially since she was someone that you knew from the past."

I narrowed my eyes, trying to hold down my anger. "Look, Jeff. I don't know what all this bullshit is about, but I had no idea that she worked for the company I called to come and clean this house."

"But I gave you a list of companies and asked you to decide which one. Isn't it ironic that you chose the company where she works? It doesn't add up, especially since she decided to come back later that day."

"Isn't it ironic that, by now, my foot ain't in your ass? I don't care if it adds up to you; it adds up to me. Sounds like this is your problem, not mine. I don't like this shit you trying to put off on me. You know damn well that the only reason I allowed her to come back in here was because I thought she probably forgot something."

Jeff smirked, obviously putting on a front for the cameras. He stepped a few inches away from me, as I had moved closer to confront him. "What did she forget? I didn't see her leave here with anything."

"If you must know, she forgot to tell me something. What she left here with was closure."

"I don't understand why you're getting upset. I'm doing my job, and as I see it, you broke the rules. Anyone who breaks the rules will be asked to leave. In an effort to be fair to the others, that's how it's supposed to be."

My blood was boiling. I couldn't believe that he was trying to throw me out of here over some bullshit with Brashaney. I could see if I invited her to come here, but that wasn't the case. Jeff was about to catch hell if he was trying to spin this in his favor.

"Fuck all the mumbo jumbo. Did you come here to put me out or what?"

"To be honest, I need to investigate this more. I already placed a call to the young lady who was here, just to get more details. I have to be sure that you didn't know she worked for that cleaning company and you didn't ask her to return that night."

"Do your investigation and do it well. If you don't thoroughly investigate this, and you come back with a conclusion that is not in line with what I'm telling you, we gon' have ourselves a serious problem. Now, if you don't mind, I need to get back to something or someone who is way more interesting than you."

I walked away, but stopped in my tracks when I heard Jeff call my name. "Within a week, like it or not, Jaylin, that's when I'll be back with my decision."

I kept it moving and made my way back into the living room. Jada wasn't there anymore, so I chilled on the couch. Jeff walked by, and when I looked up, he asked if anyone was in the restroom. All I did was shrug. I had nothing else to say to a sly motherfucker I definitely didn't trust. I knew my instincts hadn't failed me. Something was up.

Feeling frustrated about the breaking news with Brashaney, I went to go look for Chase. I found her by the poolside chilling and reading a book.

"Come on," I said to her. "Let's get this going."

She laid the book on the table and slowly sat up. "Get what going? What are you talking about?"

"Put your shorts on and you'll see."

I walked away to the basketball court. Minutes later, Chase came onto the court with me. She had on a hot pink bikini top and black stretch shorts that covered her bikini bottoms. The shorts display a sizeable gap between her legs and her hair was pulled back into a ponytail.

"Where are your tennis shoes?" I asked. "Go get them so we can play a game of one-on-one."

Chase folded her arms across her chest. "I don't play basketball, Jaylin, so why waste the time? If you're looking for a competitive game, I think you may want to call Roc out here."

I bounced the ball on the ground, then took a shot and missed. "Not interested in playing with Roc. If you win, I'll cook dinner for you."

"No, if I win, you're going to do much more than cook dinner. You're going to feed it to me too."

"Bet. Now, go get your tennis shoes."

She walked off and came back ready to go. We worked up a sweat playing basketball, but after taking several shots, Chase hadn't made one. I figured she wouldn't, but it was relaxing to see her body dripping with sweat. It was also interesting to see the cheeks of her ass bulge out of the shorts. She kept pulling her shorts down, but they continued to rise to the occasion.

"You, at least, have to give me credit for trying," she said. "Some credit, and just so you know, I'm a big fan of turkey burgers."

She took the shot and finally made one. She jumped for joy and so did her breasts.

"Turkey burgers are my favorite as well. I hope you have fun making them for us. That one shot can't save you, baby. This game is over."

I took the shot and watched the ball roll slowly around the rim before dropping in. I swiped my hands together. "Done deal. And thank you very much for showing me your skills."

Chase knew exactly what I was referring to, and after retrieving the ball, she tucked it underneath her arm. She came up to me with a grin on her face.

"I got dinner for the winner, and I'll be more than happy to feed it to you. But the really important question is, do I shower first, do you, or do we shower together?"

I didn't hesitate to answer. "You go ahead and make that move first. I'll go afterward, and by then, hopefully, my food will be ready."

Chase threw the ball at my chest and I grabbed it. She walked away, so I turned to take another shot. I didn't see if I'd made it or not, because she yanked on my arm, swinging me around to face her.

"I'm sorry," she said. "But I've been dying to do this."

She hiked up on the tips of her toes and pulled the back of my head toward her. Our lips touched and tongues danced. It didn't take long for our kiss to get intense. So intense that I lowered my hands to squeeze her plump ass. I aimed my hardness in a spot where she could feel it, but this time she backed away.

"If you want to join me, the bathroom door will be unlocked. If not, I'll see you at the dinner table."

Chase sashayed away, but with so much on my mind, I stayed outside and continued to hoop. At least thirty or forty minutes had gone by before I headed inside. When I entered the kitchen, she was there talking to Jada. I suspected Chase was getting ready to make our food, and without saying a word, I went to the bathroom to take a cold shower.

Roc

"That's some foul shit," I said as Jaylin sat in one of the lounging chairs telling me what Jeff had said earlier. "You should have knocked him out cold for gettin' at you over that dumb shit."

"You know I wanted to, but I'm gon' let his ass do his so-called investigation. I can promise you this, though. If he comes back in here telling me I got to leave, all hell is going to break loose."

"I feel you, and whatever happens, you know I got yo back. I'mma call that fool out on his shit, 'cause we not gon' play the game like that. I don't blame you for gettin' your clown on, but maybe after he clears things up with yo ex, everything will be cool."

Jaylin nodded, watching as I sucked in heat from the joint I was smoking. I couldn't help myself from smoking. Desa Rae complained so much about my weed habit that I'd slacked up a bit. I didn't realize how much I missed this shit or how much it relaxed me, until these past few weeks. I must admit that the stuff Prince left behind was fire. It calmed my nerves and prevented me from rushing out of here to go put my foot in Desa Rae's ass for letting Reggie in her house.

I couldn't get over our phone call that day. And then for Vanessa to tell me that she'd seen Desa Rae with another man really messed me up. Had she been getting it in like that while I was away? I couldn't help it that my thoughts of her doing some freaky shit behind closed doors were stirring in my head. I thought about her laughing with that nigga Reggie, and I got hyped about it. It didn't seem like she had been missing me as much as I had been missing her. What if that fool was in my bed with my woman, making love to her? Anything was possible, especially since I wasn't there to see what the fuck was going on.

Then, maybe I was feeling a bit insecure, knowing that I hadn't been one hundred in this house. I'd had some close encounters with Chase that left me feeling bad behind my actions. The touchy-feely mess between us wasn't good for my relationship with Desa Rae. But what she didn't know wouldn't hurt. At the end of the day, my insecurities could very well come from all the dope I'd been smoking. I couldn't depart from my crazy thoughts, possibly because my mind wasn't right. But too fucking bad. Until I made a move from this house, the weed stayed right with me.

Jaylin and I were waiting for the women to finish dinner. Chase said she was cooking turkey burgers for her and Jaylin, and Jada said that she would throw down for me and her. We had scrapped the schedule, especially since every time I cooked, the food managed to burn. When Jaylin cooked, his meals weren't fulfilling, so it was good to see the li'l mamas step up and take charge in the kitchen.

"I'm ready to get my grub on," I said to Jaylin as he seemed to be in deep thought.

He finished the remainder of his Remy, then stood up. "Yeah, me too. Are they done cooking yet?"

"Let's go see."

I smashed the tip of the joint, putting it out with my fingertips. Then we headed inside to see what was up. Nothing. We couldn't smell nothing but air freshener. Jada and Chase were sitting at the kitchen table lollygagging and laughing as they talked.

"What's up with the food?" I raised my voice. "I thought y'all were supposed to be in here cookin'?"

"We were about to get started, loud mouth," Jada hissed. "But we got sidetracked."

"Sidetracked by what? Conversation?"

Chase rolled her eyes at me. "Excuse me, but the last time I checked, if a man wants you to do something for him, he needs to lower his voice and ask politely. You're coming off all wrong, Roc. That kind of attitude doesn't move me one bit."

Chase was starting to irritate the fuck out of me with her smart-ass mouth. There was serious trouble lurking in her future.

"Baby," Jaylin said to her. "I am hungry as hell. Would you and your fine-ass friend next to you mind cooking a brotha something to eat? I would surely appreciate it, and I promise to do any and everything you ask me to do. That's if it's within reason."

Chase smiled, but Jada's face fell flat. "Your promises ain't worth two cents, but I like the way you called me fine. That I am, so I'mma get started on fryin' up some greasy pork chops, smothered in a bunch of thick brown gravy with onions and peppers. Potatoes, too."

"Bake my pork chops, if you don't mind. I prefer pork chops instead of turkey burgers," Jaylin replied.

"This ain't the early 1900s, sweetie. I don't take orders, so therefore you will have to eat whatever we cook for you. If you don't like it, you already know what to do. Chase, do you want to remind him or shall I?"

Chase sauntered over to Jaylin and sat on his lap. "That would be for you to eat an apple. However, since you have been so nice to me, I will scrap the turkey burgers and bake your pork chops. Your potatoes will not include salt or butter. Deal?"

"Not really, but it depends on how the food looks. I may have to consider that apple."

"Tuh," Jada shouted from behind the counter. "Then more food for us."

Chase looked over at me and cut her eyes. I didn't know what the fuck her problem was, but her anger was directed at the wrong one. After mean muggin' me, she went into the kitchen and got busy with Jada. Jaylin and I stayed at the kitchen table, playing several hands of spades. He was up in the last game, but I ended it as soon as dinner was finished.

"The least y'all can do is set the table," Jada said. "Jaylin, get up!"

"Talking to me like that will not get action. Besides, I'm not sure if I'm going to eat anyway."

He got up from the table to go look at the food. While wincing at what Jada had made, she lightly pushed him. "Oooo, I swear you make me so sick. I can't believe how picky you are, and I bet you drive your maids crazy. How many of them do you have anyway?"

"I don't have any maids, but the woman who cooks for me does a much better job than you do."

"Well, that nappy-head bitch ain't here, is she? Your insults are workin' me, Jaylin. If you don't like what you see, don't eat it."

The gaze in Jaylin's eyes damn near shot Jada dead. "If you call anyone else that I mention to you a bitch, I'm going to repeat exactly what Prince did to you. You've been warned. Watch your mouth."

Jada made her body shiver. "Brrrrr," she said with sarcasm. "Your words are cold and I'm so scared. You can trust and believe that if you put your hands on me, I'm gon' cut yo tail up, Jada Mahoney-style. Now, move away from me. I'm exhausted from cookin,' and I'm not in the mood for any noncents."

"Nonsense or noncents?" he asked, still fucking with her.

"Nonsense or cents," I said, intervening. "No matter what, I'm ready to eat."

"Me, too," Chase added. "Resolve y'all issues later."

Jaylin refused to eat what Chase had cooked too. She was upset. He went to the fridge and pulled out an apple and some cottage cheese. With a disgusted look on his face, he removed a box of crackers from the pantry and returned to the table to sit down.

"I wouldn't feed my worst enemy that shit Jada cooked. Who in the hell put pork chops in that much gravy and grease?"

"Obviously, yo mama didn't, mine did," Jada said, then looked at me. "Roc, if you would like more than just two pork chops, you're welcomed to it. That ole cheese and cracker eatin' fool over there don't have a clue what good cookin' is. His loss, not mine."

No gripes from me because, as usual, the food looked good from where I was standing. Jaylin could get down on that apple and cottage cheese all he wanted to; I was doing the chops. I helped Jada set the table so we could eat.

"Before we eat, let's give thanks for this wonderful food I done prepared for y'all, while Chase did nothin' but run her mouth and stand around lookin' cute. I don't want her to get any credit when y'all sink y'all's teeth into my chops."

"I did bake one pork chop and I also smashed the potatoes," Chase said. "I have no problem giving credit where it's due. You did your thing, so let's pray, especially for you."

I wasn't about to back away from praying and listen to Jada's mouth. I bowed my head with the others. I closed my eyes, but nobody said anything.

"Roc," Jaylin said. "Gon' and do your thing. Show leadership and express how thankful you are for all of this mess."

"Excuse me, Jesus," Jada said, opening her eyes. "But fuck you, Jaylin, all right? You gon' make me go there with you durin' prayer, so please be quiet for one doggone minute."

I hurried to speak so this wouldn't go on and on. "I'm very thankful that Jada knows how to throw down, and I'm thankful that as hungry as I am, I didn't have to dive into any of Chase's horrible food. Thank you, Lord. Amen."

"Amen," the others said, except Chase.

"Screw you too, Roc," she said. "You're working me."

"Not yet. But I will, though. Soon."

Like a brat, she kicked me from underneath the table. I guess she expected for me to scream like a scared li'l bitch, but all I did was display a wicked smile.

"You scare me when you look at me that way," she said with sarcasm in her voice. "Please stop."

"You should be scared. Very scared."

She threw her hand back at me. "Don't fool yourself, Roc. I'm not afraid of anyone, so you can save those dirty looks for another day."

"My looks don't have nothin' to do with this. And I'm not goin' to sit at this table and tell you plenty of reasons why you should be afraid. I'll mention one. It's because I'm tellin' you that you should be."

Jada dropped her fork and wiped her mouth with a napkin. "All these threats are killin' me. Since when do men do it like that? I say if you gon' do somethin' to somebody, then gon' ahead and do it. Stop talkin' all that noncents and show, not tell."

"Nonsense," Jaylin said, chomping down on his apple. "N-O-N-S-E-N-S-E. Stop sounding like an idiot."

"Yo M-A-M-A, momma. She's the only idiot I know of, for havin' someone like you."

Jaylin sat across the table from Jada without saying another word. There was a crisp silence for about a whole minute before he got up and stroked his goatee. I thought he was leaving the kitchen, but when I saw him grab Jada's hair from the back, it shocked the shit out of me. He pulled tight, causing her to squeeze her watery eyes.

"Let my hair go," Jada shouted, trying to remove his hands by scratching at them. That made him pull tighter.

He bent down and calmly whispered in her ear. "I'm gon' say this one more time, and you'd better listen to me good. Leave my fucking mother out of your mouth. You can play all you want to with me, but going there will get you in a neck brace. That's no threat, baby, it's a promise."

Jaylin pushed her head forward, before letting it go. Afterward, he removed her plate from in front of her and dumped it in the trash. Before Jada could process what he had done, he also dumped the remaining pork chops on the stove in the trash.

"Hold the fuck up!" Jada shouted. "Oh, no, you didn't just pull my hair like that and dump my food, did you?"

Jaylin folded his arms and stood defensively. "Stop talking and do something about it. Ain't that what you said you were sick of people doing? Talking with no action."

"This is so uncalled for." Chase dropped her fork on the plate. "These damn men in here need to grow the fuck up."

Yes, I was irritated, so I tore into her. "Bitch, who you talkin' about? You don't have nothin' to do with what's goin' on between them, but you had to throw me up in the mix. Get the fuck out of here with that grow up bullshit. Grow yo ass up."

Jada rushed into the kitchen. She tried to open the silverware drawer, but Jaylin blocked her. "If you find a knife, you'd better know how to use it," he said.

They argued over him blocking the drawer, and Chase quickly got after me. "I'm not going to be another one of your bitches. From what I gather, you already have one who got your sensitive-ass tripping. Leave me the hell alone and go somewhere and find another joint, weed-wacker."

I tried to be the better person here, but that didn't always work for me. Ladies I respected. Hoes with smart mouths were on my chopping block. But instead of putting my hands on Chase, I smacked her plate off the table, causing it to crash on the floor. The shattering glass caused Jada and Jaylin to stop arguing. They looked to see what was up.

I stood and pointed at the food on the floor. "Since you like being on your hands and knees, I figured you wouldn't mind. Eat up before I shove somethin' else in your foul-ass mouth to keep you quiet."

Chase's jaw dropped wide open. "I swear to God that I have never met a man as disrespectful and lowlife as you."

Jada chimed in, too. "I have and he's standin' right here." She looked at Jaylin. "These tantrum-throwin' niggas done lost their damn minds. All I gotta say is nobody better be sleepin' peacefully up in here tonight. Better sleep with three eyes open, because it's on and poppin'."

Jaylin looked at me and nudged his head toward the door. He appeared as frustrated as I was. These dizzy-ass broads had crossed the line. It was time to get them the fuck out of here.

"I can't do this much longer," I said to Jaylin as we stood in the game room. "Somebody about to get hurt up in here. I don't know who the fuck they think they are."

"I feel you on that, but calm down. You've been upset since your conversation with Desa Rae, but being like this ain't gon' help us one bit. I know the situation at your place of business got you on edge too, but if we play our cards right, this will all be over with soon. The last thing we want to do is put the ladies in a position to win. When we start losing control, that's what will happen. So, take a deep breath and get your head on straight. I almost lost it my damn self. Jada know she be tripping, and it took everything I had not to punch her ass."

"Both of them be trippin', and I ditto what you're sayin'. I'm gon' laugh my ass off when I see Chase packin' up her shit, and all I'm gon' say about Jada is I will surely miss the food."

We laughed and started to shoot pool. Jaylin bent over to take a shot.

"FYI, don't go to sleep tonight," he said in a teasing manner. "Jada will have that knife by her side, and there is a chance that my dick may get cut off or yours."

He shot the ball into the hole, then waited for me to take my turn. "Jada gon' mess around and find herself asleep in a casket. I'm not goin' to sleep until she does, but she ain't the only one who will have a knife in their possession. What's good for her will definitely be good for me."

Jaylin agreed. We didn't finish shooting pool until later that night.

Jada

I didn't care how fine he was, how big his dick was, how well defined his body was or how smooth his conversation was. Jaylin was a hot-ass mess, and he had no clue how to treat a real woman like me.

I couldn't believe that he pulled my hair like that. My scalp was screaming. He lucky I couldn't get into that drawer to get a knife. I would have cut him up in a thousand and one pieces, but then again, talk was cheap. What threw me for a loop was the argument between Chase and Roc. They were going at it tough. When I asked Chase about it, all she said was angering him was in her plan. I didn't see how his dissing her was in the plan, but for now I had a plan of my own. My plan was stalled because Jaylin and Roc hadn't gone to sleep yet. We were all in the bedroom with the lights still on. Roc sat shirtless against the headboard while playing a video game on a handheld PlayStation. Chase lay sideways in bed. She was underneath most of the cover while paging through a fashion magazine. Jaylin sat shirtless against the headboard too. No cover was on him, and he was reading *The 48 Laws of Power*.

With Sylvia being gone, I was on the edge of her bed polishing my toenails. It was almost two in the morning. I figured that Jaylin and Roc didn't want to go to sleep because I'd threatened them earlier. Any other night, they'd be out by now.

I yawned right after Roc did, then I glanced at the wall clock. It ticked away as we chilled in silence. After another ten minutes went by, Chase cleared her throat.

"Jaylin, I don't mean to bring this up, but I'm curious about something. If you don't want to answer my question, you don't have to."

"What?" he said without looking away from the book. "What are you curious about?"

"About why Jada mentioning your mother upset you earlier. I didn't peg you out to be a woman beater, but you were pretty hot."

I sat silent because I wanted to hear his response, if he was willing to give one. He kept reading and didn't respond until he flipped the page. "Correction. A woman beater I am not, and I don't get down like that. Calling my mother out of her name or speaking of people that you don't know nothing about angers me. I lost my mother when I was young. Needless to say, I don't like it when anyone disrespects her."

"I can understand that," Chase said. "How did you lose your mother?"

"She was murdered. Now, if you don't mind, I'd like to get back to reading this book."

"I'm sorry to hear about your mother and thanks for sharing. Maybe Jada will feel compelled to apologize, and maybe you will also apologize for grabbing her hair."

Apology my ass, I thought. I wasn't sure where Chase was going with this, but Jaylin ignored her last comment.

"Hey, Roc," I said. He kept playing the video game, but nodded his head. "Why did you get all bent out of shape when Chase called yo woman a bitch? Are you gon' take issue with everybody who calls her out of her name, or don't you realize that words are just words and sometimes people say things out of anger?"

Roc set the PlayStation on his lap. "We all say things out of anger, but I take some shit personal. When you start talkin' about the people I love, I got a problem with that. Say what you want about me, but don't cross the line with people who ain't here to defend themselves. That's all I'm sayin'."

"Exactly," Jaylin said.

The room went silent for a few more minutes.

"Riddle me this," Roc said, looking in Jaylin's direction. "Why yo ass ain't asleep? I know I'm tired as fuck, but I'm not about to wake up with half of a dick."

Shoot! He must have spotted the scissors I had tucked underneath the mattress.

"I don't think nobody is that stupid to cut off your manhood," Jaylin said. "But if you lose half of your dick, whoever is that bold should lose a titty."

Ouch. That hurt just thinking about it. I wasn't going to use the scissors to go out like that, but I was going to go into the closet and go to work on Jaylin's expensive clothes. As pricey as they were, I was sure he'd be mad. But after hearing about his mama, maybe I was in the wrong for saying what I did.

I turned sideways to look at him. "I'm sorry to hear about your mama, and I apologize for speaking ill about her. I know how it feels to have a parent murdered. My father was murdered right in front of me when I was seven years old. It's somethin' I'll never forget."

Truthfully, I didn't know my father, but I'd heard that's what had happened when I was three, not seven. Chase touched her chest. "That's horrible, Jada. I couldn't even imagine seeing anything like that. Did you know the person who killed him?"

"Yep. It was his best friend. He used to come to our house all the time. I really liked him. Then my father and him got into it one day, and the next thing I saw was him pullin' out a gun and shootin' my father. Shot him twice in the face, then in the chest. That's why, to this day, I don't have too many people I consider friends. To hell with friends."

Jaylin turned the page in his book and still hadn't said anything. Roc was the next one to open his mouth. "That's messed up, Jada. When I was younger, some similar stuff went down with me and my parents. My Uncle Ronnie had to raise me. I don't think I would've preferred it any other way. I guess some things happen for a reason."

"I didn't experience anything like that with my parents," Chase said. "But as I mentioned to Jada before, my father was the worst person ever. I wish I had the guts to kill him when I was younger, but I could never go through with it. Eventually, he died from cancer. I never forgave him for what he did to me. It's not as painful for me to talk about it anymore. Years of therapy helped me realize that none of it was my fault. I used to blame myself, but now I know better. I've also had plenty of struggles with relationships, but that wasn't all on me either. Some men are downright trifling dogs who don't give a care about women."

"I agree with you on that," I said. "I've had my share of those kinds of men as well."

I was still waiting for Jaylin to say something, but he hadn't said one word.

"Jaylin, did you hear what I said to you a few minutes ago?"

He kept his eyes glued to the book, refusing to look away from it. "I heard you, but I'm not in the mood for a group therapy session. If I was, I'd go seek counseling in private."

I swear his funny-acting ways truly amazed the heck out of me. Where in the hell did he come from?

"Well, everybody can't afford to pay four and five hundred dollars an hour for a shrink, so we have to sit around with regular ole folks and get some shit off our chests. Thanks for listenin' Roc and Chase. I'm takin' my ass to sleep before I have to go off on somebody."

I fluffed my pillows and pulled the cover over me. Minutes later, Jaylin put the book down and stretched.

"Truth is," he said. "We all got stories to tell from the past. Some of us more messed up behind that shit than others, and as I see it, y'all are really some screwed-up people. But therapists or not, we got to keep on living our lives and try to make the best of it. There is no future in living in the past, and playing the victim of your circumstances will only delay your progress. I shouldn't have pulled your hair, but I did. It won't happen again."

"I agree with what you said, but that wasn't an apology, was it? I'mma need you to try that again."

"And I'mma need somebody to turn out the lights so I can go to sleep," Roc said, pulling the cover over his head. "We can pick up where we left off tomorrow."

Chase yawned and put the magazine on the floor. "I know, right? I'm tired, too."

She pulled the cover up to her neck and rested her head on the pillow. I got up to turn off the lights, but still wanting an apology from Jaylin, I jumped on his bed. I bounced up and down on him and purposely elbowed him in the chin for pulling my hair.

"Daaamn, girl." His voice was strained as he tried to push me off of him. "Get yo heavy butt off my stomach."

"Not until you apologize to me. Until then, I'm stayin' here all night."

Jaylin stopped pushing me and dropped his arms to his sides. I straddled the top of him and could feel his monster madness between my legs. I'd be lying if I said it didn't feel good.

"Jada, get up," he said in a calm manner. "And don't think that I can't get you off of me."

"Go ahead and try."

I continued to bounce on his midsection. I swear *it* was growing! I swear!

"If I try, you're going to be on the floor."

I threw my hands in the air and kept bouncing. "Wee, look, Jaylin. No hands."

He couldn't help but to blush, but kept threatening to push me on the floor.

"One. Two," he said.

On three, I assumed we would hit the floor. If I was going down, he was going down with me. When "three" spilled from his mouth, I tightened my arms around his neck and held on tight as he tried to shove me away from him.

"Help," I shouted in the partially dark room. A sliver of light was coming from the closet and I remained on top of him. "I'm not lettin' you go until you apologize."

Jaylin tried so hard to push me away from him, and it wasn't long before we wound up on the floor, playfully tussling. I couldn't believe that it was so hard for him to apologize.

"Say it! I can't hear you," I teased.

"Then clean your ears out, because I already said all that I'm going to say. Let my neck go and get in the bed. I'm exhausted from wrestling with you and I need some sleep."

I finally let go, but bumped into Chase when I got up.

"I thought you needed my help," she said.

"I yelled that out quite some time ago. You're too late."

She laughed and screamed when Jaylin snatched her up and tossed her on the bed. He put all of his weight on top of her, causing her to strain as she tried to catch her breath and speak.

"Uhh, pleeease, get uuuup..... I can't breathe."

"What's that?" Jaylin said. "I can't hear you. If you came to help Jada, then you haven't done much of a good job."

Chase laughed and pleaded for him to get up. He did, but to no surprise she managed to work her way on top of him. Bitch. I was kind of mad that she came over to so-call help me. Instead of tripping, though, I grabbed a pillow off my bed and made my way over to Roc. I lifted the pillow in the air, but before I came down with it to hit him, all I heard was, "Back up, li'l mama. Don't you even think about it."

After that, he slammed his pillow into my stomach. I doubled over and he tore me up with pillow punches. We wrestled with each other, and it was quite fun rolling around on the floor with him. I touched every part of him that my hand could reach. All he did was laugh it off.

"Stop," he kept saying. "You trippin', ma."

Maybe I was tripping, but so was he for touching my ass. That was in bed, of course, as I lay in his arms and sighed. I couldn't help but to think about our little confession session tonight.

"It's apparent that we all got issues, but as they say, prayer changes things. We don't be praying enough, and y'all ain't prayed since Sylvia got booted out of here."

"Speak for yourself," Jaylin said. "You may not see me doing it, but I do so everyday."

"I do it most of the time," Chase said. "But there are days that I do skip."

I looked her way with shame in my eyes. "You shouldn't do that Chase, 'cause out of all of us, you're the one who needs more prayer than anybody. You need to be on your knees everyday, and I don't mean on them to give blowjobs."

Roc and Jaylin busted out laughing.

"Forget you, Jada. You need prayer way more than I do. I can't believe you think otherwise. I'm going to pray for you, just for thinking that. Your mind couldn't be right after that comment."

"My mind is very right, but I'm not gon' get into it with you over yo lack of prayer. No matter what, we all need it, some way more than others."

Trying to lead by example, I got out of bed and got on my knees. Roc was quiet like a mouse. I could see him looking at me. I had to pull his non-praying self on the floor with me. His face was twisted; I couldn't believe how irritated he looked. It was apparent that his mama and daddy hadn't taught him a thing.

"Boy, that is a real ugly face, so stop lookin' like a scorned child. Don't you know that God can see you? You'd better wipe that look off yo face, 'cause I don't want to be nowhere near you on Judgment Day. Today could very well be it, who knows?"

Roc put one finger on his lips. "Be quiet. You talk too much. I do pray, but maybe not as much as I should. I'm frownin' because I'm tired."

"Jesus was tired too, but he didn't let that stop him from saving you. Put on yo happy face right now. Let Him see how thankful you are for your blessings."

My eyes dropped to Roc's goods. There was no doubt that he had *a lot* to be thankful for. I cleared my dirty mind, and as he kneeled next to me, Chase and Jaylin also kneeled next to their beds.

"Are we doin' this out loud or what?" Roc asked.

"Silently," Jaylin replied. I agreed.

We all prayed silently for a few minutes. With my eyes closed, I prayed for my family and friends, for people around the world who I didn't know and for everyone in this house. I also prayed for me to win this challenge, and I asked for God to give me strength to cut back on the fatty foods I'd been eating. I seriously needed to lose weight, and the last thing I needed was for my health to become an issue. I felt Roc move, and when I opened one eye, I saw him get in the bed. I finished with an "Amen" and followed suit.

Jaylin was still on his knees, but shortly after me, he returned to his bed. Chase, however, remained on her knees.

I whispered to Roc, "I told you she needed all the prayer she could get. That girl needs some work. Big ups for her."

Roc looked at me with a smirk on his face. He put his hands behind his head and closed his eyes. Less than two minutes later, I could hear light snores. I looked at Chase who was still on her knees.

"Psst, Jaylin," I whispered. "Shake her shoulder and see if she done fell asleep. She must be sleep, because it don't take that dog-gone long to pray."

Right then, Chase lifted her middle finger, but kept her eyes closed.

"Ooo, you gon' get it. Who gestures something like that when they're in the middle of prayin'? You need some serious help. I'mma get back on my knees to pray for you again."

"Shut up. Please," Chase shouted, then opened her eyes. "I can't even pray in peace."

"It shouldn't take that long for you to pray for sex with men out of wedlock. No matter how long you stay on yo knees, God ain't goin' for that mess. I doubt that yo prayers will be answered, so you just wasted a whole lot time. Now, goodnight, people. See you all in the a.m."

I punched my pillow and got comfy in my own bed. I looked over at Roc resting peacefully and was sure to keep my distance. When he had to answer for his sins, I didn't want to be nowhere near him. No siree.

Chase

Last night was fun. I was glad that we were able to put our differences aside from earlier. I slept in the bed with Jaylin, and as he held me in his strong arms, I sure did feel safe, sexy, and secure. But now wasn't the time for any attachments. Time wasn't on my side and the moment had come for me to make a move.

Jeff had become a true pain in the ass. He was starting to bug me about seeing him again. While in the bathroom, I whipped out the cell phone, whispering through it.

"Jeff, how many times do we have to go through this? Nothing else can happen between us until I leave this house. You have to be patient with me. I promise that all good things come to those who wait."

"I don't mind waiting, but I don't like watching you interact with Jaylin and Roc. It seems as if you're enjoying yourself a little too much. Must you sleep with Jaylin every night? You do have your own bed."

He offended me, but I didn't have time to deal with him right now. "Again, it's all in the plan, Jeff. Please don't be upset with me, okay? I appreciate everything that you've done for me, but I won't be able to pull this off without your cooperation. Please tell me now that I can still count on you to be there for me. I'm starting to get worried."

"You can trust me, for sure. I need for this to hurry up and be done with."

"Well, we're on our way to the finish line. Have you decided what you're going to do about Jaylin's situation yet?"

"Yes, I have. I'll be there the day after tomorrow to tell him what I decided."

"Are you going to tell me?"

"No, not yet. But I'll just say that my decision is going to surprise you."

"Great. I love surprises. Now, I must go. Before I do, let me remind you again not to get upset by my actions. Just remember the real reason behind all of this."

"I will. Be careful and call me if you need anything else."

I ended the call with Jeff and couldn't help but to call him a sucker underneath my breath. The one thing I hated was a weak-ass man who sniffed behind me. I wanted a hard brother who would stand up to me at any time, yet love the hell out of me. I admired the way Roc was when it came to Desa Rae. She should be very grateful for her man—for now. High or not, touchy-feely or not, he was the kind of man who had no problem protecting the woman he loved. He defended her to the fullest, and I had to give him some credit for trying to stay on the right path. It wasn't easy being in this house with a woman like me; an aggressive woman who was willing to go after what I wanted. Roc's attempts to fight me off were applaudable, but unfortunately for him, he was starting to lose that fight. I could sense that something was about to change. He was upset with Ms. Desa Rae and it showed all over his face. His anger was now directed at me because I was an easy target. I was capable of easing some of the hurt he felt inside and that was the real reason he was mad at me. Without even knowing it, he played right into my hands. I'd seen broken-down, neglected men in these situations plenty of times before. It was on me to lift their spirits and offer them some in-the-meantime hope.

That was exactly what I was going to offer Roc. I wasn't sure if I was more excited about my future plans with him or with Jaylin. Surely, only time would tell.

Since we had hit the sack so early in the morning, most of us slept until almost noon. Jaylin was the only one who got up around seven. I'd already had breakfast, worked out and showered. During breakfast, I asked Jada if she would braid my hair. She agreed to do it. We spent most of the day in the living room, watching TV while she braided my hair. The braids were medium-sized long braids that were styled into a ponytail. They were long enough for me to wrap in a neat bun. I even asked her to leave a few strands dangling, and she said that she would.

As for Jaylin and Roc, they'd been in and out of the house all day. I saw them drinking and shooting pool in the game room earlier. When dinner time passed, they saw that we were still busy, so they whipped up sandwiches for all of us.

"Thanks," I said to Jaylin as he passed me a plate with a sandwich and some chips. He gave Jada a plate, then opened a can of soda for her.

"Is there anything else I can get y'all?" he asked.

"Nope," I said with a smile. "Thanks."

Jada thanked him. Then she invited him and Roc to watch a movie with us after dinner. They agreed to, but when the movie got started, Jaylin kept on yawning.

"I need to go take a nap. My body can't function properly on four hours of sleep. With the lights off in here, it's hard for me to stay up."

"Aww, boo," Jada said. She was already finished with my hair and was relaxing on the couch. "This movie is so good. I hate that you gon' miss it."

"Give me an hour, maybe two, and I'll be back."

Jaylin left and went into the bedroom. Roc stayed, but he kept yawning too, while rubbing his forehead.

"Are you okay?" I asked him.

"I got a headache. But this movie got me hooked, so I'm chillin'."

"Would you like for me to go get you some aspirin?"

"Yeah, that'll work. I appreciate it."

Not minding at all, I got up to get Roc some aspirin. I stopped in the kitchen for a glass of water, and then gave the water and aspirin to him.

"Thanks, ma."

"Anytime."

Jada stood, already knowing that if Jaylin was out of the room, she was supposed to jet and give Roc and me some privacy. She cleared her throat and stretched. "I'm goin' to join Jaylin in the bedroom. My bed is callin' me right about now."

"Good night," I said, waving.

Roc didn't say a word. He was still into the movie. Jada left us alone, and that was when I scooted in closer to Roc on the couch.

"You don't mind me getting this close, do you?"

"Nah, you good."

We sat in silence watching the movie. I was so disturbed that his attention was on the movie, but I definitely knew how to direct his attention elsewhere. I picked up an already rolled joint that Jada had left in an ashtray on the table. I put the joint in my mouth, letting it dangle. After reaching for a lighter, I flicked it to light a flame.

"What you know about that?" Roc questioned.

"I know more than you think I do."

I took a puff from the joint, and as soon as smoke filled my mouth, I swallowed to fill my lungs. Shortly thereafter, I choked and my eyes watered. I couldn't stop coughing, so he hit my back and laughed.

"That shit is potent. You can't hang with the big dog, ma."

"Obviously not," I said between coughs.

Roc took the joint from my fingers and began to explain how I was supposed to show love to the joint.

"First, you gotta wet yo lips real good, like this." He licked his thick lips, then pressed them together. "Then you gotta treat the joint with love and respect. Hold it steady with the very tips of your fingers and stare it down. Bring it to your lips and kiss the tip of it. Gently place it between your lips, then slowly, real slowly, inhale that shit. Let the smoke fill your mouth and close your eyes. Use your tongue to stir the smoke around before you swallow. Like this."

Roc displayed what to do, looking sexy as ever as he showed love to the joint. I was turned on, and after a few more hits, he passed the joint back to me. I did exactly as he'd told me, but this go around I took my time swallowing. He cheered me on.

"There you go, ma. That's how you do that shit."

I took another puff, then another. I could feel my eyelids getting heavy, but the feel of Roc's arms around my waist was more satisfying. I gave the joint back to him, watching as he finished it off.

"I feel so, so light," I said, giggling.

"That means it's workin'."

Roc stood and removed his wife beater. He left his navy sweatpants and tennis shoes on.

"It's hot as hell in here," he said. "That air conditioner ain't about nothin'."

"Even if it was, I'd still be hot."

Following Roc's lead, I stood to remove the tank shirt I had on that was cut above my midriff. I also took off my jeans, leaving me in my nude-colored bra and panties. The room was partially dark, but he could definitely see how spectacular I looked. His eyes narrowed as he sat back on the couch, continuing to look me over.

"I wasn't talkin' about yo kind of hot. Put your clothes back on before you start somethin' up in here."

"That's what I'm trying to do. And just because I define being hot differently than you, don't be mad at me."

I straddled Roc's lap to face him. My arms fell on his broad shoulders, but his hands remained still.

"I'm not mad at you, but we need to cool out with all these teasin' tactics."

"Okay. How about you cool out and I go ahead and do me?"

Roc's lips were clamped shut as I slithered down to the floor and got on my knees in front of him. I moved in between his legs and tugged at the string on his sweatpants.

"Why you fuckin' with me, ma?" His voice was soft. "You already know what's up."

"Yeah, I do. All I'm trying to do is relax your mind, and for one day, relieve you of some of the overwhelming stress you've been under."

He didn't respond, so I assumed he was down for whatever. I carefully eased his dick out of his sweats, watching as it flung out long, thick, and hard as a rock. No doubt, the Viagra pill I had given him was working.

I secured his pipe with both hands, then dropped my head into his lap to give him pleasure. His muscle stretched my mouth wide. Deep throating him was near impossible, but all eleven inches of him was covered with my dripping saliva. Roc couldn't keep still. He squeezed the back of my neck and pumped my mouth like it was a juicy pussy.

"Daaaam," he responded in a whisper. "Do that shit, ma. You straight up doin' it."

I planned to do it, but not with his sweats on. I backed away from his goods to lower his sweats. Roc helped, and once he was naked, he removed my panties and bra. He returned to the couch; I got back on my knees. With his foot propped on the coffee table and his other leg stretched on the couch, I had easier access. I scooted in between his legs, and this time, I added his balls to the mix, rolling them around in my mouth. My slick hands massaged up and down his shaft, but his head received most of the attention.

"Mmmm," Roc moaned. "I'm about to turn loose on yo ass. Then it'll be time for me to bust that pussy wide open."

I never thought he'd go there. Then again, yes I did. I hurried to bring him to my justice, and when I did, he filled my mouth with his liquids. I swallowed, yet Roc remained tense as ever.

"Fuck," he shouted while squeezing his muscle. "This mutha-fucka feelin' hyped."

He was so right about that. It didn't take long for him to get hard again, and right after he put on a condom, he laid me on top of him in a sixty-nine position. I didn't mind giving him more head, but when I felt his cool breath blow on my coochie lips, it tickled.

"Your turn." His tongue slithered inside of me, and he flicked my clitoris so fast that I tried to jump away from him.

"Ohhh, shit," I screamed out. Hopefully, Jada and Jaylin would think it was someone in the movie hollering, not me. "Go deep inside, Roc," I moaned and pleaded. "My clit is too sensitive, and… I want to feel your big dick."

He ignored me. The only things that eased inside of me were his cold fingers that he circled and jabbed to bring down my juices. I was so sticky and wet, and all I could feel was him lapping on my pussy juice like a thirsty dog. I swear I wanted to cry, but the tears didn't come then. They came a few minutes later when he laid his warm body on top of mine and wrapped one of my legs around his back. With my foot flat on the floor, Roc circled his chunky head around my hair-free slit, then pushed every inch of his hardness inside of me. My eyes grew wider and so did my mouth. It felt like a bolt of electricity had ripped through my body, causing it to stiffen.

"What the hell?" I hollered out in so much pain. Roc had a massive dick, and with it being on super hard, it was difficult for me to tackle. I could barely move with him inside of me, but he stroked me like a professional. For the first time ever, I felt like an amateur.

"Say you're sorry." He began to stroke harder. "That you're sorry for treatin' me ill."

I didn't want to apologize, but as he pushed deeper into me, my pussy felt battered. Much pain was in my stomach and I squeezed the muscles of his ass, as I gasped for air. I strained to tell him how sorry I was for going off on him. "Very sorry, and it will never happen again."

Roc kissed my cheek, but he didn't let up. "Never again, huh?" he said. "I don't believe you."

"Please do," I cried out. "You have my word."

"Your word ain't shit. Good thing your pussy got it goin' on though."

I wanted him to ease up, but it didn't appear that was going to happen. His strokes, however, were backed up by a rhythm that tickled the shit out of my insides. To calm my shakes, I took deep breaths and scratched down his muscular back with my long nails. That made him slow down a bit, but not for long. He removed my legs from around his back and placed them high on his broad shoulders. This time, he was so deep in me that I couldn't move if I tried to. I tightened my fist, and with each thrust, I bit down on my lip, trying my best to hang.

"This hurts," I whispered. "But it still feels so good. Slow it down, though, and take your time with me. I'm not going anywhere but right here, okay?"

Roc gazed into my eyes, then he pecked my lips. His lips smacked my cheek, and he moved his mouth to my ear, licking around it. "I haven't broken you down yet, so I know it hurts. It should, and there are consequences for hurting my feelings."

I couldn't say I was sorry enough, but what I could say was Roc had been fucking the shit out of me. Somehow or someway I had to get control of this. My breasts wobbled around from his speedy thrusts and I kept grunting, moaning, and groaning.

"Rooooc," I whined. "Let's move into another position."

Giving me some relief, he lowered my legs from his shoulders, then pulled out of me with ease. I felt so much wetness dripping between my legs and down the crack of my ass. Ready for more, I turned on my stomach.

Roc proved that he didn't have a gentle bone in his body. He smacked my heart-shaped ass, as I backed it up to him, and spread my cheeks so he could enter me from the back. With each thrust, he pushed me forward. I fought back—well, pushed back—and began to work him too. Thing is, he was too strong. He manhandled the hell out of me, and needless to say, I was defeated. My toes curled, my breathing increased, and my next orgasm brought about one big creamy mess between my legs. I was spent after that, but to no surprise, Roc wasn't. He lifted me from the couch and sat me on the coffee table. I was still a sticky mess, but that didn't stop him from opening my legs. He sat in front of me and picked up the lighter. A flame flickered in front of his handsome face.

"What are you doing with that?" I asked.

"Shhh," he said, then picked up the joint. "Rest back on your elbows and let me cool things off."

I leaned back on my elbows, watching as Roc took two hits from the joint. He held the smoke in his mouth, then leaned into my pussy and slowly released the smoke. Some of the smoke escaped in the room, but the way he blew on my coochie made it feel good. He did it one more time, but the last time, he blew smoke inside of me. Then, with a long drag he sucked me as if he were bringing smoke back into his mouth.

"Pussy and weed, ma. That's what energizes me."

This was some straight up thug shit! I was outdone, yet totally impressed. My legs trembled, and as I pushed my feet against his chest, he grabbed my ankles. He stared at me through hooded eyes, and then stood to hold my legs apart. I remained on the coffee table, wondering where he would venture to next. My pussy was already high from all that he'd put into me, but he still wasn't done. I almost regretted giving him the Viagra.

"Stand up, face the couch and bend over," he ordered.

Roc was high as hell. I wondered if he would remember any of this tomorrow.

"Are you giving me orders now?"

"No. And let me correct myself. Please bend over and face the couch."

He let go of my ankles, so I got into the position he requested. He stood behind me, and lifted his foot on the couch. Again, he went in with force that left me barely standing on the tips of my toes.

"Who in the fuck let you out of the house?" I said, but got no answer.

No answer, but pure satisfaction as Roc massaged my breasts and went for his first gentle move of the night. He bent over and placed a trail of delicate kisses down my back.

"Hold on tight," he said in a calm voice. "Magic is about to happen."

I knew what that meant, only because I felt his dick thumping inside of me. We were on the verge of coming together, but he threw me off guard when he used his strength to lift and balance my legs on his thighs. I used my hands to hold me up on the couch, while he drove us into overtime. When all was said and done, I fell to the couch and rolled on my back. Dizzy, I squeezed my eyes and held my stomach.

"Exhausted?" Roc asked.

I opened my eyes and saw him standing over me. "Very. I need a cold shower and a bed."

"You ain't no fun. And next time, if there will be a next time, I'mma need for you to put in a li'l more work."

He smiled, then lightly brushed his fingertips between my breasts, placing something between them. When I looked at it, it was the Viagra pill I had given to him earlier.

Surprised that he didn't take it, I quickly sat up and tried to explain.

"See, I thought that giving you this would make you feel hyped and—"

Roc placed his finger on my lips. "Shhh. I know what you thought, but you were wrong. I don't take pills that are given to me by others, so now you know. Like I said, all it takes is good pussy and weed to get me hyped, but I've had enough of both. What happened here tonight stays between you and me, ma. Yo cherry was sweet, but I busted it. After I hit the shower, I'm hittin' the bed. By mornin', all of this will be forgotten."

Roc walked off, leaving me alone in the living room. I looked between my legs, and sure enough, he had murdered my pussy. That big-ass dick tore me up. I wasn't so sure about this staying between us, though. I still had a competition to win.

I looked at the clock, seeing that it was a little after eleven. For the next forty-five minutes or so, I watched TV, then went into the bathroom to take a long shower. Once I was done, I wrapped a towel around me and entered the bedroom. There was a lot of snoring going on. I knew some of the snores were coming from Roc, because I'd gotten familiar with his snores. Jada was getting it in too, but I couldn't quite hear Jaylin. He was a light sleeper, so I stood at the end of his bed, looking at his sexy body that outlined the sheets. I pulled on the sheets, trying to wake him. He didn't move until the sheets got near his midsection and exposed his chest. That was when he sat up.

"Chase?" he questioned while squinting.

"Yeah, it's me. I couldn't sleep and I wanted some company. I thought you said you'd be up in an hour or so."

"I planned on getting up, but that sleep had me in a coma."

"Well, I'm glad you're up now. Are you going to get up and join me?"

Jaylin sat silent for a few seconds and stroked his goatee. "Yeah, baby. Give me a minute, all right?"

I smiled as I made my way to the door, gearing up for round two and ready to set the roof on fire.

When Chase woke me up, she brought me back to reality. The reality was I had been curious to see what was up with her. I felt well rested, and since everyone else had shut it down, it was time to creep.

I quietly made my way out of the bedroom and into the bathroom to take a leak. Right after I flushed the toilet and washed my hands, the bathroom door squeaked open. Chase walked in, still holding a towel around her. I hated for people to interrupt me while I was in the bathroom.

"I said give me a minute, didn't I?"

"Yeah, you did. But for whatever reason, I couldn't wait much longer."

Chase closed the door, then dropped the towel. All was forgiven, as I studied her silky, naked body that had curves in all the right places. She didn't have that thickness in her thighs, how I normally preferred it, but there was a gap that was very inviting.

"So, I assume you like my hair," she said. "Jada did a great job, didn't she?"

The direction of my eyes shot up to her hair. "Yeah, uh, you hair looks nice."

"But."

"But what?"

She turned around, displaying her backside. "But my ass looks a whole lot better, doesn't it?"

I studied her ass before commenting. "Yes, your ass is just right, however, I know you didn't come in the bathroom to show those cute dimples on your ass to me, did you?"

She smiled and moved closer to me. "Yes, I did, but I also wanted to show you more than that."

Chase sashayed over to the shower. She slid the glass door aside, then turned on the rainfall showerhead. The shower was the only good thing about this bathroom, but now that Chase was in it with me, that made things even better.

"Come inside and wash me," she offered, then reached out to give me a bottle of shower gel.

"Honestly, my intentions were to take a seat on the counter and watch you for a while."

"That's no fun and that won't help me one bit. I prefer to have it my way, that's if you don't mind."

I believed in compromising with women, so why not give the woman what she wanted? I stepped out of my silk pajama pants, grabbed a condom from the medicine cabinet, and then joined Chase in the shower. Only a few feet separated our naked bodies, allowing me to get a good view of her. I dropped the condom on the seat and squeezed shower gel on the sponge. Chase was surprised that the first place I washed was her face. She touched my hand to stop me.

"You can do much better than that, can't you?"

Giving me a hint, she turned and raised her arms in the air. I moved in closer and pressed my body, particularly my dick, against her backside. I reached around to her front side and started to wash her breasts. As I covered them with soap and warm water, I also massaged them together. Chase's nipples grew from my touch; her breasts felt firm as ever. Much of the water spraying from the showerhead was dripping on her, so it quickly washed the suds I created down her slender body and into the drain. I circled the sponge around her midsection, but before going down low, I leaned in to her neck and lightly sucked it. She released soft moans, until my sucks turned into tiny bites. Her moans got louder—obviously, the bites aroused her more. She reached up and started to wiggle her fingers through my curls. I loved when women did that to me, especially Nokea. I shook her from my thoughts, then I inched the sponge down lower, stopping right at Chase's pussy. She separated her legs and that was when I let go of the sponge. I cleansed her insides with my thick fingers, digging them deep into her and wiping her walls. Almost immediately, I could tell Chase damn sure was no virgin.

"I can tell that you've had much experience with sex." I felt how loose she was.

She quickly fired back. "Experience with a bunch of vibrators and dildos. But no experience with a man like you or with one who has measured up to your size."

That was bullshit, but she didn't have to know that I knew it was. I moved her forward to face the wall. The water now poured on both of us and it was up so high that we got drenched. I wasn't ready to sample the goods yet, so I continued my foreplay by pressing my lips down her backside.

"That tickles."

She laughed as I squatted to kiss her entire ass. I massaged her cheeks, then took several quick swipes at her asshole to get a reaction. She sucked in a deep breath, then released it.

"I don't know how much more of that I can take," she said. "But I must tell you that I'm enjoying every minute."

I stood to put on the condom, deciding to save her pretty ass for later. Chase turned to face me and that was when I lifted her to my waist. She secured her legs around me and placed her arms on my shoulders. We exchanged an intense stare, before our lips finally met up and brushed against each others. The smacking got louder as more water dripped between our sloppy kisses. The taste was sweeter than a cherry.

"Mmmm," Chase moaned between breaths. "You're a damn good kisser. Why...why do I feel like I've known you forever? That you're about to make love to me, Jaylin, instead of fuck me like most men will do."

Sometimes, it was best to keep quiet and listen. This was one of those times, so I let Chase speak her mind. Besides, I was speechless, and the feel of her hotspot had my mind elsewhere.

She felt light as a feather. It didn't take much for me to position her in my arms and direct my hardness into her heat. As I entered her, she shut her eyes and tensed up. A sigh followed, then she relaxed.

I turned my hips in slow circles and began to paint her walls with long strokes. Her grip had gotten tighter around my neck. She held on to me as if she didn't want to let go. I couldn't believe when I looked into her eyes and saw them turn glossy. So many women were extremely emotional during sex, but I had an idea what was going in Chase's mind. She attempted to hide her emotions, but that was when I pressed my lips against a corner tear to wash it away. I halted my strokes, but continued to secure her in my arms.

"Are you all right?" I asked. "Did I hurt you or something?"

She moved her head from side to side. "No, Jaylin. You're not hurting me at all. I enjoy looking into the richness of your grey eyes. Please continue."

Her smile put me at ease. Little did Chase know that after hearing what her father had done to her as a child, I knew that she was fragile. I had to be careful how I handled her. Every woman was different. The way I had sex with them was determined by what I knew about them. She didn't need for me to be aggressive, as her father had already been that. I was pleased that she appreciated my approach.

I backed away from her insides and lowered her trembling legs. When I sat on the seat, Chase straddled the top of me and latched her pussy onto my shaft. Her insides were deep and warm, making it easy for me to move around in. We rocked our wet bodies together, and it wasn't long before she shouted out that she was coming.

"I feel it coming, Jaylin."

She bounced a little faster while on top of me. To help her juices flow, I used my fingers to massage her stiff bud that peeked through her slit. My dick swiped against her bud at the same time and I felt it swell. Shortly thereafter, her body went limp and it felt as if she'd melted in my arms. I held my arms tightly around her so she wouldn't fall backward. To calm her, I covered her breast with my mouth and circled her nipple with the tip of my tongue. My dick remained inside of her, because in no way was I ready to call it quits. Neither was Chase. This time, she turned around to ride me and bent over far enough where her hands touched the floor. With each thrust, I lifted myself from the seat, trying to leave my mark on every corner of her pussy that I could. My hands rubbed down her perfect curves that sculptured her waistline, and I couldn't get enough of touching her sweet ass. I narrowed my eyes to watch it jiggle on top of me, but had to shut them so I wouldn't be forced to come. She wanted me to come. I could tell by the way she was popping it.

"How does it feel?" she asked me. "I know how it feels to me, but you tell me."

"I don't tell until I'm done."

She laughed and sat up straight with her back facing me. I now had better access to her pearl that I could feel above her widely stretched slit, thanks to my muscle that had it stuffed to capacity. As she rode me at a slow pace, I manipulated her pearl again. I used my other hand to squeeze her breast, and to be honest, it had been a long time since I'd felt this relaxed.

"We're perfect for each other," Chase said softly. "I love the way you play with me and your gentle touch is about to make me come...come again."

She put her fingers on top of mine and assisted me in toying with her. We rubbed and massaged her pussy together. I was feeling this shit, and with the condom still on, I felt her juices rain down on me.

A look of pure satisfaction was on her face as she turned toward me and got on her knees. She backed up to where most of the water poured and asked me to come to her. I got up from the seat, removed the condom and stood in front of her. She took several squeezes on my ass, then opened her mouth wide to receive my dick that was now harder than a black diamond. With water dripping over my lashes, I looked down at Chase, trying to swallow all of me. Her hands were turning around my shaft and she paid extra attention to my head. It was damn sure a pretty sight to see such a beautiful woman like her go to work on me. Her jaws tightened and her soft moans, along with the feel of what she was doing made me roar.

"I'm about to show you how good this feels in a minute," I strained to say.

Chase's mouth was too full to reply. My legs got weak, so I sucked in my six-pack and then let a deep breath escape. I held her head steady and began to stroke her mouth faster. I could feel my muscle sliding far down her throat. That was what finally made me show her how pleased I really was. Chase washed away my sperm with her mouth, before standing to face me.

"Before morning gets here, I guess we'd better wash each other up for real," she said. "The water has turned cold, and just so you know, that was a lot of *feedback* that you gave me."

"I was saving it for you, but there's still so much more left. I don't know what else I want to do with it. Do you have any suggestions?"

Chase got closer and put her arms on my shoulders again. She got on her tippy toes to give me a kiss.

"I know plenty of things you can do with it. And I'll give you my suggestions after we wash each other."

This time, she put shower gel on the sponge and asked me to turn around. The water turned colder, but the way she washed all over my body felt relaxing. There was no doubt that we still had a long night/morning ahead of us. Chase Jenkins had definitely put something on me that I would remember for quite some time. Or should I say, at least for another week—maybe two.

As the guilt for what I had done started to kick in, I tossed and turned until I finally fell asleep. When I did, it felt like I was in a coma.

There I was, standing at the altar in my black tuxedo, looking dope as ever. The church was filled to capacity with Desa Rae's family and friends, as well as mine. My boys were lined up beside me, and we all watched as my beautiful daughter, Chassidy, made her way down the long aisle, dropping flower petals along the way. I couldn't help but to smile because she reminded me so much of Desa Rae. We had a lot to be proud of and today was no exception. It was special, no doubt. After everything that Desa Rae and me had been through, our wedding day had finally arrived. The woman who I loved was about to be my wife, and no words could explain how nervous I felt inside.

Minutes later, the "Here Comes the Bride" theme played. Desa Rae appeared at the back of the church. I could barely breathe—her beauty had taken my breath away. The cream-colored strapless dress she wore was silk. It rested perfectly on her healthy curves and cut right underneath her knees; the dress allowed everyone to get a glimpse of her smooth legs and high-heel shoes that matched her dress. Twisted pearls were gathered around her neck, and her hair was full of loose curls that fell on her shoulders. I had never seen my woman look so fabulous. She had gone over and above the call of duty for this day. Every eye in the church was glued on her, especially my boys, who all stood in awe.

Desa Rae moved slowly down the aisle with a blank expression on her face. No smile was visible whatsoever. I wondered why she wasn't smiling; I definitely was.

By the time she reached me, several tears had reached the rim of her eyes and poured over. She handed me her flowers to hold while she wiped her tears. I had a handkerchief in my pocket, so I pulled it out and wiped her tears with it. I was surprised by the continuous flowing of her tears because Desa Rae wasn't one to always show her emotions. Everybody waited for her to gather herself, but she couldn't seem to do it. Trying to calm her, I stepped forward to hold her in my arms.

"I know, ma," I said. "I'm excited about this day too, but you gotta stop cryin', so we can get this show on the road."

She backed away from me and gazed into my eyes. "Why, Roc?" she asked. "Why did you have to do it?"

I quickly blinked and was caught off guard by her question. My heart dropped to my stomach. I could feel beads of sweat dot my forehead.

"Do what? What are you talkin' about?"

"You know darn well what I'm talking about. How long have you been messing around with another woman?"

Several gasps could be heard throughout the church and a few snickers too. I couldn't even move. It felt like cement had been poured over me. I stared at Desa Rae, in shock that she was standing before me accusing me of being with someone else.

"Answer me, damnit! Open your mouth and answer me," she demanded.

I suspiciously looked around, trying to play down the noise she was swinging my way. "May...maybe we should go somewhere and talk in private. We really don't want to put our business out there like this, do we?"

She smacked away a tear that had fallen. Anger that I had never seen *before crept across her face. "I don't care if anyone hears what I have to say. And if you refuse to come clean, this shit is about to get real ugly."*

It had already gotten ugly to me, especially with so many people in our business. What was it that she expected me to say? I hadn't been with no other woman, other than the one incident I'd had with Chase. There was no way that Desa Rae had found out about what had happened during my Hell House stay. I wasn't so sure where she was going with this.

I reached out to hold her, but she wouldn't allow me to touch her. "I think you're makin' a big mistake. I haven't been with anyone. Why are you trippin' so hard, ma? When I tell you it's the wrong time and place, I really mean that shit."

Desa Rae swallowed hard and pointed her finger at me. She spoke through gritted teeth that made me take a few steps back. "You owe me the truth, bastard. You said you loved me, and I'm going to ask you this one more time. Who have you been having sex with?"

By now, I had tuned out everybody. I reached out for her again, trying to talk some sense into her, but she wasn't having it.

"I'm here to marry you. I haven't been seein' nobody else, so why are you accusin' me of somethin' that ain't ever happened?"

Desa Rae pulled out a letter from inside of her wedding gown and unfolded it. Before reading it, she sighed and gazed at me with a pained look in her eyes.

"One week ago, I went to the doctor. His office called yesterday, the day before our wedding, and told me that I needed to come in to discuss the results of my tests. My test for syphilis came back positive, Roc. If you've been faithful to me, please tell me how something like this could've happened?" She waved the letter in my face. "Explain this crap to me. I'm very fucking confused right now."

I was so embarrassed. When I looked around, not one single person had left. They wanted a response too, but I was speechless. I'd used a condom when I had sex with Chase, and I knew for a fact that it didn't come off. We did, however, indulge into a lot of sucking on the private parts, but the chances of me catching anything from going down on her was slim to none. Or, that was what I'd thought. Then I thought about Desa Rae getting her freak on with someone else. I wasn't sure what was up with her, but in no way would I stand at the altar and confess to what I'd done.

"I honestly do not know how somethin' like this could've happened, but when is the last time you hooked up with Reggie? You did have sex with him, didn't you?"

I tried to swing that shit back her way, but Desa Rae reached out and slapped the living daylights out of me. My head jerked to the side, and I rubbed my cheek, trying to soothe the hard blow.

"How dare you bring Reggie into your mess? I trusted you, Roc. I trusted that you would finally do right by me, but you just couldn't do it, could you? You couldn't keep your dick in your pants, and now you done gave me a disease that one of those trifling bitches you've been screwing with done passed on to you. You stand there with your lies and think it is okay for you to ruin my wedding day. You ruined this day for me, and I want you out of my life for good!"

I kept shaking my head, saying no. The people in the church were loud, but nothing was louder than a cackling laugh that came from the back of the church. When I turned to see who it was, it was Chase. She laughed uncontrollably and clapped her hands.

"Way to go, Roc," she shouted. "How's that marriage thing working out for you?"

"Not so good," Desa Rae said. I felt a jab in my stomach, and when I looked down, she had stabbed me with a knife. I tried to tell her I was sorry, but the pain in my stomach prevented me from saying anything. She smiled and backed away as I tried to break my fall by clinging to her dress. I fell to my knees, but before I hit the floor, the dream came to an abrupt end.

I quickly sat up in bed with a sheen of sweat covering my fore-head. That dream had me messed up, and when I looked at the alarm clock, it was almost seven o'clock in the morning. It was another day, yet I wasn't guaranteed another dollar. Not unless I started making some noise in here to get the others out and get my ass home. Chase was first on the list. I planned to have a talk with her today about why I thought she should leave. I was positive that she'd see things my way.

Before I got out of bed, I looked at her bed and she was lying there out like a light. I guess I didn't have to wonder why; maybe because I had knocked her back out and she was still in a coma. The dream had me feeling horrible about fucking her, but a part of me felt as if it was justification for the way Desa Rae made me feel when I called home. She should've known better. I didn't play that kind of shit, and shame on her for thinking that I was the kind of man she could toy with. At the end of the day, what she didn't know wouldn't hurt. No matter what the hell I had dreamed about, what had happened between me and her had to stay a secret.

I took a lengthy shower, especially since I did a quick wash-up last night. I then gave myself a clean shave. When I tossed the blade in the trashcan, I saw several used condoms. The one I had used with Chase was in the kitchen's trashcan, so these condoms had to belong to Jaylin. If not, Jada and Chase were around here doing some freaky shit that didn't make sense. I smiled from the thought of Jada and Jaylin fucking. That was what made sense, especially since they were always playing with each other and hanging around together.

"Dirty dog," I whispered underneath my breath and laughed again.

I exited the bathroom, dressed in purple and yellow B-ball shorts and a Nike tank shirt that showed my tats. I was somewhat lazy today, so I didn't feel like working out. Instead, I stopped at the computer to check my fan mail. There was a lot of it, but I was so eager to find out what had happened between Jaylin and Jada that I only replied to one email from Cadeesha in St. Louis.

Roc, I swear that I've been all over St. Louis looking for you. LOL. I'm a forty-something-year-old woman who dates younger men. Your relationship with Desa Rae is so interesting, and I would like to know, from you, what makes you and Desa Rae's relationship work, considering the big age difference?

I had to think about this. After last night, it was obvious that it wasn't working well at all. But I had to give the woman some hope— keep some for myself too—even though there could possibly be serious trouble in paradise.

Cadeesha, what up, ma? If you search hard enough in the Lou for me, you'll definitely find me. Right now, I don't know how my relationship with Desa Rae is working, but I'm hyped about it. I don't believe the success that we've had revolves around our ages as much as it does around two people who understand each others needs, who know the real meaning of compromise, and we recognize that neither of us are perfect. A person can be any age to realize that, so don't be skeptical to date brothers the same age as you. I happened to luck up on a woman who is willing to work with me, especially at a level that I need for her to be. Wish me luck, 'cause after this Hell House challenge is a wrap, I'mma need all the support I can get. You know how much I love trouble, so say a li'l prayer for Black Love. It's still alive, so never give up on it.

I hurried to shut down the computer. On my way to tease Jaylin about what had gone down between him and Jada, I stopped in the kitchen. I picked up three slices of bacon that Jada must have already cooked. I put the bacon between a buttery biscuit and added grape jelly. I stuck the sandwich in my mouth and jetted to the workout room.

From a distance, I saw Jada and Jaylin inside. He was showing her how to lift weights. They seemed chummy and turned their heads when I opened the door.

"Morning, Roc," Jada said with a big, bright smile. "I see you couldn't wait to get your hands on my homemade biscuits. I got up real early to make those, especially for you."

"Aww, that was sweet," I teased. "I don't have to tell you that you did your thing. You know a nigga appreciate it."

"You'd better. Jaylin in here tryin' to show me how to quickly shed some pounds. He says that liftin' weights is a good start, but what you got to say about that?"

"I say you're on the right track, but all people have different results. You may lose more weight by doin' aerobics."

"Yeah, that too," Jaylin said. "But more than anything, you gon' have to cut your calorie intake in half and exercise a whole lot more than what you're doing."

"I'm not gon' cut my calories by much, but I will try to exercise more."

Jaylin wasn't trying to hear that. "If you don't cut your calories, then you're defeating your purpose for losing weight."

Jada got defensive. "No, I'm not. I heard that people can burn off all calories, no matter how many they eat, by exercisin' for thirty minutes every day. Like, look at Michael Phelps. I heard he eats close to ten-thousand calories a day. He's skinny as a pencil, and all he do is swim."

"Swim a lot," Jaylin countered. "A whole lot, where he can afford to eat like that. You, on the other hand, can't."

"And you, on the other hand, need to stop insultin' me before I shove my foot up your you-know-what."

"No, I don't know what that is." Jaylin seemed to have an attitude and he backed away from her.

Jada sat on the weight bench, pouting.

"I'm only trying to help you," Jaylin said. "Stop wasting my time and don't come crying to me again because you gained seven pounds since you've been here."

"Six," Jada said, standing up. She went over to the treadmill and got on it. "Six pounds that I'm getting ready to walk off right now."

"Well, prepare yourself to walk until midnight. Six pounds ain't coming off like that."

Jada rolled her eyes. "Thanks for the inspiration, fool."

Jaylin ignored her and returned to the weight bench. I guess a night of sex wasn't capable of bringing him and Jada together.

"You ain't working out this morning," Jaylin said to me.

"Nah. I had a long night and my energy level ain't up to par right now."

"I feel you on that. Same here. Mine ain't either. I had a real long night and even a longer early morning."

"Nothin' wrong with that, especially if it was worth losin' sleep."

Jaylin lifted the weights over his head and smiled. "No doubt, it was worth it. Well worth it."

I nodded, not expecting for Jada to satisfy Jaylin sexually. He seemed like a hard man to please. Then again, Jada had a wild side to her that she probably kicked up a notch during sex. The visualization in my head didn't quite do it for me, but I had to take Jaylin's word for it being worthy.

I finished my sandwich and sat on another weight bench to watch TV. Jada had headphones on and loudly sang lyrics to a song. The singing was distracting and I couldn't hear the TV. So instead of hanging around, I decided to chill outside on one of the lounging chairs. I was outside for about fifteen minutes before Jaylin swooped in to take a seat. He wiped sweat from his face, then tossed the towel over his shoulder.

"So, what's the play for the day," he said. "The football games are starting at noon and the Eagles are playing the Steelers. It's supposed to be a good game. I can't wait to see what's up."

"Same here. I hope Jada and Chase find something to do so they don't be buggin'. Maybe Jada will stay on that treadmill until midnight. That may not be such a bad thing."

Jaylin agreed. Anything to keep her mouth shut and out of the way.

"She's a feisty-ass something," Jaylin said. "Every time I tell her something for her own good, she gets defensive. I guess some people don't like to work out, but she should know better, especially since she likes to eat all those fattening foods."

"Right. Maybe she still tired from the workout she got last night, or early mornin', as you put it. That may have been enough workin' out right there."

"Slaving in the kitchen to make biscuits ain't exactly what I call a workout. And she'd only been lifting weights for fifteen minutes before you came in."

"I wasn't referrin' to her workin' out in the kitchen or in the exercise room. I was talkin' about the other action that went on last night. I saw several condoms in the trash. Somebody must have put in some overtime. Pounds had to shed."

Jaylin licked his bottom lip and rubbed down his goatee. "I forgot to throw those in the other trashcan. My bad."

There was a newspaper on the table, so he picked it up and started to flip through it. Minutes later, Jada busted out of the workout room huffing, puffing, and limping.

"Whew," she said, fanning herself with her hand as she came over by us. "I've had enough! That working out mess ain't for me. How do y'all stay in there for hours at a time? I got hot and too sweaty."

She dropped in a chair. Jaylin lowered the paper and looked over at me. "Man, please respond to her so I don't have to. After five minutes, she shouldn't be that tired. That's a damn shame."

"I know, ma. You did more sweatin' than that last night, didn't you?"

"Not as much sweatin' as you probably did," Jada said, then winked at me. "What time did you and Chase finally hit the sack, or in other words, wrap things up?"

I sucked my teeth. "It took a while, but we got there."

"You sure did, especially from the way she was hollerin'. You must have gotten all the way up in there, and I applaud the bitch for climbing up that tall ladder and staying on it."

I laughed wickedly as I thought about Chase pleading for me to stop. I surely put it on her, but my intentions were to keep what had happened between us a secret. Jada, however, kept at it. Jaylin had also put the newspaper down and was tuned in.

"Was it good, Roc?" Jada asked, playfully shoving my shoulder. "Or did she put it on you?"

"Nah, she definitely didn't put it on me. Not at all. As for it bein' good? It was good, not great. I'll leave it there."

"Oooo," Jada said in a giddy mood. "I can't wait until she wakes up so I can drive her! You mean to tell me that she didn't leave you with no everlastin' memories? She must not be a full-blown sista then. We usually leave men with unforgettable memories."

"Let me repeat myself, it wasn't bad. It's just that some people can't be matched when it comes to sex."

Jaylin cleared his throat and massaged his hands together. "Let me get this straight. Are you saying that you had sex with Chase yesterday?"

I made myself clear. "Nah, fool. I'm not sayin' that I had sex with her yesterday. What I'm sayin' is I knocked her muthafuckin' back out and tore that shit up."

"Damn!" Jada shouted. "Be blunt with it, why don't you? Is this how men talk amongst each other? I see how y'all get down, and I'm all ears!"

Jaylin sucked in his bottom lip and bit it. "So, yesterday, as in last night, you were intimate with Chase? Do you mind telling me what time all of this took place?"

I felt like I was being interrogated and cocked my head back in straight up confusion. "Does all that matter?"

"Not really, but I want to know."

"Why?"

Jaylin placed his hands behind his head and let out a soft snicker. "Why? Because I exchanged juices with Chase last night too."

Jada threw her hands up in the air and pursed her lips. "Who cares, Jaylin? Now ain't the time for you to be talkin' about you and Chase exchangin' orange or apple juice. I'm tryin' to get the scoop about her and Roc. Finish telling us, Roc. What else happened?"

I tried to ignore Jada. My face fell flat. Jaylin's words almost knocked the wind out of me. Maybe I misunderstood him, like Jada had done.

"Juices, as in sexual juices?" I questioned.

Jada snapped her head in Jaylin's direction. "Boy, shut yo mouth! Are you sayin' that she climbed up your long ladder too?"

"Fucking her is not exactly what I did. I'll just say that we slapped naked bodies together all night and well into the early morning."

I was in disbelief. "So you fucked her?"

"Roc!" Jada shouted again. "Yes! Get a clue, 'cause it obviously sounds like he did. That's just nasty and triflin'. Ugh."

I was straight up shocked. I could tell by the look on Jaylin's face that he was taken aback as well. How in the hell did something like this happen? I wasn't mad, but something inside of me wanted to hurt Chase. I'd be wrong to go inside and confront her, though. I wondered if Jaylin was thinking the same thing. I thought back to the condoms I'd seen, still thinking that he'd knocked Jada off in the process.

"Uh, I gotta say that I'm kind of fucked up in the head right now. But didn't you have sex with Jada too?"

Jada pointed to her chest. "No, not me, stupid. Chase! Didn't that man just tell you that he exchanged Kool-aid all night and all mornin'? What about that do you not understand?"

I put my hand up to Jada's face. "Silence yourself. You're annoyin' me. All I'm sayin' is somethin' don't add up."

"It doesn't add up to me either," Jaylin said. "But what's done is done. Now we both know that there is major work to be done here."

Jaylin scooted back from the table. His face looked a li'l tight with anger, but before he stood up, the sliding doors opened and out walked Chase. She was dressed in a tight pencil skirt, stilettos, and a fitted shirt that cut above her midriff, making her breasts appear even bigger and rounder. Her braids were in a neat bun and two strands dangled near each side of her face. She looked sexy as hell as she swished her hips from side to side, heading our way.

Jada rushed up to her with her hands in the air. "Girrrl, give me a high-five, 'cause that's how you do that shit! I'mma be sure to give you my number so we can talk! I need to hear every single detail about who was slangin' dick the best and how they got down. I mean, did you see any fireworks, shootin' stars, or red lights?"

Chase had the audacity to giggle and give Jada a high-five. She then walked over to the table and removed her sunglasses.

"What a lovely day," she said, squinting at the sun. "I feel like a million dollars and I wanted to thank the two of you for showing me such a good time." She squatted next to me and held my hands with hers. "From day one, I knew we would click. And if you ever want to get my pussy high again, or murder it as you clearly did, please look me up. From the bottom of my heart, Roc, I really do view you as a decent man. My only hope is that your woman wakes up and realizes the same thing."

Chase stood and paraded over to Jaylin. He ignored her and pretended to be checking out the newspaper. "Yeah, I know you won't say much to me, but just so you know, my time with you almost made me rethink this whole thing. You were extremely good to me, Jaylin. God knows if I could package up your dick and sell it, I would. I was so touched by the way you comforted me, but I think we both know that as passionate as our time together may have been, love doesn't live in our hearts anymore. Too many people have hurt us, and we can't go there with the love thingy anymore. That's too bad, huh?" She bent down and kissed his cheek. He still didn't move. "For now, fellas, I must go. There is nothing else left in this house for me to do, and quite frankly, I'm getting bored. So be good for me. If either of you want to hook up when you leave here, I'll be easy to find."

Neither of us responded. Chase sighed and shrugged. She wiggled her hips to straighten her skirt, then walked off. Jada stopped her and they exchanged a few words. That was when Jaylin looked at me and I shot him a glance too.

"Crazy bitch," I said. "I guess she don't realize that she did us a favor by leavin'."

"Maybe so," Jaylin added. "But I'd go further than that. Crazy, bad bitch that may bring about some trouble. All I can say is watch your back."

He lifted the newspaper, reading it as if he wasn't fazed one bit. Either he wasn't or he was a good actor and deep down he was feeling like I was—like shit.

The whole day had been messed up. I was pleased that Chase had left. All I kept thinking about was her laughing in my dream, and how the whole day started off on the wrong foot after that. Jada and Jaylin were in the kitchen arguing about dinner. To be honest, that shit got on my nerves. I tried to ignore them, but it wasn't always easy to ignore Jada's big mouth.

"I said let me cook it," Jada said, trying to push Jaylin away from the oven. "I won't cook your steak all the way through. If you want blood runnin' out of the doggone thing, so be it."

"All I said was make it medium. Just a little pink in the middle, but still tender. I didn't say medium rare."

"All I know is done or undone. If you want to get into all of that medium stuff, then you may have to stay in here to cook your own steak. Just stay out of my way. Shoot."

Jaylin did his best to stay out of Jada's way, but with her dancing around in the kitchen, and singing, it was kind of hard to do. I sat back on the couch, watching TV with my feet propped on the table and my hands behind my head. I wasn't that hungry, but the aroma moving in from the kitchen smelled pretty good. Jada always wanted me to taste her food, so she rushed into the living room area with a slice of steak on the tip of a fork. I opened my mouth and chewed on the juicy piece that left my mouth watered.

"Is there anything yo ass can't cook?" I asked. "Damn, that's good."

A grin was locked on Jada's face. "I know, right? The only thing that I can't cook is Hamburger Helper. It doesn't help me at all, and I can never get my noodles to cook right. Other than that, I'm good. After I win this money, I may even open up a restaurant. Help me think of a name, okay?"

"Dream on, ma. Those restaurant doors won't open if you're expectin' to win this challenge."

Jada winked at me. "Oh, we shall see."

She walked away and came back with a piece of paper in her hand. She put it on the table in front of me and gave me a pen. "Here. Sign this before I forget."

I removed my feet from the table and sat up straight. "What is it?"

"It's a waiver. A waiver sayin' that you relinquish all rights to Chase's pussy and you don't want no more of it. I think this may come in handy for the future." She turned to look at Jaylin in the kitchen. "Jaylin, you may need to come sign this waiver too. If not, y'all may be indebted to that pussy forever. I'd hate to see that happen."

Jaylin ignored Jada. I balled up the paper and got up to throw it in the trashcan. "Please don't discuss that bitch with me. And joke or no joke, the shit ain't funny."

"Ohhh, so now she's a bitch? Did you call her that when y'all were fuckin' yesterday? I bet her name was Cinderella then."

Jada had no idea how much she was irritating me. The look on my face said it all, but she kept at it.

"Man, pay her no mind," Jaylin said, as I stood in the kitchen drinking water. "You know she ain't got it all."

Jada's attention went right back to Jaylin. He, however, picked up his plate and carried it over to the table. After cutting into his steak, minimal red juices flowed.

"Ugh, that's nasty," Jada said, hovering over him with a frown on her face. "That steak looks undone to me. How can you eat somethin' like that?"

"Let me give you a lesson about food that you may not know.

When you don't cook your steak all the way through, it can help fight heart disease. You have much more taste and the juices stay locked inside. Nutrition wise, a steak like this is good for you."

Jada threw her hand back. "I appreciate the info, but I could care less about that nutrition stuff. Whoever be makin' up that stuff be lyin', and the next thing you know we'll be all dyin' from drinkin' water. Now, about those juices. If you want somethin' juicy, all you gotta do is say so. I can offer you somethin' way better than a bloody steak."

Jaylin forked up some lettuce from his salad and held it toward Jada's mouth. That was surely a good way to get her to walk away because she did.

After dinner, I had to keep myself busy or else I'd lose it. I played a lengthy game of basketball with Jaylin and shot pool with Jada. I tossed back a couple of drinks before swimming several laps in the pool. I even went to the workout room to clear my thoughts, but nothing seemed to help. By night time, I was still swoll and couldn't even go to sleep. Jada and Jaylin were knocked out, but I laid in bed, staring at the ceiling and thinking about Desa Rae. Had I fucked up? I wasn't so sure. I was starting to regret that I had asked her to marry me. What I had done with Chase was a hint that maybe I wasn't ready. But I felt ready. I wanted her to be my wife, but there was no doubt that I had to get my shit together.

Since I couldn't sleep, I got up to watch TV. I quickly got bored with that, so I sat on the couch thinking. Someway or somehow, without jeopardizing my chances of winning this challenge, I had to see Desa Rae. I had to know that everything was good, and it didn't feel right knowing that Chase was no longer here. I hated to be paranoid, but I was. I also wasn't sure how I could get out of here without anybody knowing it. There had to be a way. Yeah, there were cameras, but Jeff had to sleep. And at one o'clock in the morning, I suspected that he was knocked out.

With that in mind, I crept into the closet to change clothes. I put on a pair of sweatpants and a T-shirt. Jaylin was always up late reading something, but I was glad to see that he was down for the count. Jada was hugged up with a body pillow, and her snores implied that she wasn't going to wake up anytime soon. I closed the door to the bedroom, and just in case someone was watching me on the cameras, I played it off and went to the workout room. I stayed in there pumping iron for a while, and several minutes later, I exited from the side door. That door led me close to a fenced-in area of the yard that was secluded. I knew I could hop the tall fence, but the question was if I could manage to get to Desa Rae's house before anyone noticed that I was gone. The plan was for me to find a payphone, call my boy Craig to pick me up and take me to Desa Rae's crib. All I wanted to do was see her. I needed for her to tell me that everything was good. I also wanted to make sure Reggie wasn't creeping while I was away, so my plan was in motion. That was until I grabbed the fence. As I started to climb it, an alarm sounded off. It was so loud that it rang my eardrums. I hurried to hop down from the fence, and quickly made my way back inside. I plopped down on the couch, and minutes later, Jada and Jaylin came from the bedroom.

"What's up with that alarm?" Jaylin said, squinting as he looked outside.

Jada covered her ears. "I know. That thing is loud. Shouldn't we be callin' the cops?"

I got up and looked outside with Jaylin. "Somethin' must have triggered it. Maybe an animal or somethin'. I wonder how we can make it go off."

Jaylin shrugged, then walked outside. I did too, but Jada stayed inside. "Y'all be careful," she said as we made our way out of the door. "If somebody starts shootin,' run."

I had seriously fucked up. When Jeff showed up almost ten minutes later, he questioned us. Jada and Jaylin admitted to being asleep, but I had to come up with something, in case he'd seen me on the cameras.

"I was up late workin' out," I said. "While I was in there, I had to drain the vein, but unfortunately, I couldn't make it to the bathroom, so I stepped outside to take a leak. I stood by that fence over there. Maybe I triggered the alarm by accident."

"Probably so," Jeff said. "I turned off the alarm, but stay away from there because this house is highly secured. I immediately contacted the police to let them know everything was okay, so no worries on that end."

We all nodded. After Jeff left, we returned to bed. I guess I wouldn't get a chance to see Desa Rae until this was over. That day couldn't come soon enough. Damn!

Jada

It was truly one crazy mess going on up in here. These fools had me smoking Newport cigarettes again, and I had not had one cigarette since I've been here. Chase was already packed and gone. Jaylin and Roc hadn't said much else about her. They spent most of the day watching TV, playing video games, and eating.

I seriously wanted to know how both of them felt, because Chase did not get up out of here like Sylvia did—as a sucker. Going out like a true ho or not, Chase worked what her mama had blessed her with, like I had never seen it done before.

The looks on Jaylin's and Roc's faces were priceless. They were definitely caught off guard. Chase did the right thing by leaving. Being here would have been hell for her. Yep, they were mad because she screwed both of them in the same day. But why be upset with her? Men do it all the time. I was sure that both of them had been there and done that before. They were surprised that a female had done it and had gotten away with it. Chase made no excuses, and she damn sure didn't have to explain her actions to anyone, even though they were trifling.

I couldn't figure out why she threw Jaylin into the mix on the same day. But then again, she had been trying to get at him since day one. Maybe that opportunity became available. She told me what her intentions were with Roc, but damn. I couldn't even imagine going at it with both of them. She didn't appear worn or nothing. I'd still be somewhere sleeping and sucking my thumb.

Like I said, Roc and Jaylin hadn't said much else to me, and the games kept them occupied. The following day, however, Jeff came to the house early in the morning to deliver a package from Chase. He was in and out, so no one saw him. I hurried into the bathroom to see what was inside of the envelope.

There was a letter from Chase that advised me how to follow through with the rest of our plan. Her plan, as written, would guarantee us all of the money. I didn't realize how or why it would until I got to the end of her letter. My mouth dropped wide open. Roc and Jaylin were both cooked. I had the power in my hands, and the truth behind everything shocked me.

First of all, Roc should've known better. The moment he looked into Chase's eyes, didn't he see Desa Rae? Hell, both of their last names were Jenkins so he should have made the connection. Chase said that she and Desa Rae had the same father. It was so obvious to see that they were related, especially when I held Desa Rae's picture in my hand. I shook my head because men were always known for thinking with the wrong doggone head.

As for Jaylin, Chase said she had sex with him, simply because she wanted to. She joked about how many orgasms she had and said that if she didn't know any better, she would have fallen in love. According to her, blackmailing him was hopeless because his tricks already knew what to expect. But either way, he was a goner too. I definitely had my work cut out for me. Chase had gotten us this far, but I had to get us over the finish line.

"I'm counting on you," Chase said in the letter. *"And to keep you entertained, feel free to put this flash drive into the computer to see your girl in action."*

I wasn't sure where Jaylin or Roc was, but I tiptoed to the computer and stuck the flash drive in a slot. Almost immediately, I covered my mouth and rocked in my seat, as I watched Chase and Roc go at it. He was wearing her ass out! There were times that Chase looked helpless. If I was Desa Rae, I'd be mad as the devil. This wasn't a good look, it was a damn good look from my point of view. Roc was a bad mutha…yes he was. I was craving for him, along with the aggressiveness he brought with him. I couldn't pull myself away, and when he started smoking a blunt, I was hooked. My pussy throbbed as if he had blown smoke into me.

I kept fanning myself, unable to take much more. As I fast forwarded, the video switched to Chase and Jaylin. Oh. My. God. I stood and started jogging in place. I was too excited. I quickly peeked around the living room area, and seeing no one in sight, I rushed back to my chair. My eyes were glued to the monitor again. This shit was too sexy to watch. Jaylin didn't even have to go out like that. He was so passionate. The forehead kisses and body rubbing had me squirming in my seat. I felt what Chase had felt. She looked good too—firm breasts, and why didn't my ass look like hers? As a woman, a straight woman, she could get it. No she couldn't. Instead, I wished it were me in the shower with Jaylin. I wondered if he could lift me and hold me like he did her. Hell f-ing no, so I quickly washed the thoughts from my head, continuing to watch. After several marriages, not one of my husbands lasted more than ten minutes. Kiley was the only man I dated who could do it like Jaylin. I mean, Chase and Jaylin went at it for quite some time. In the shower, on the counter…hell, she even bent over the toilet. I was outdone as I focused my eyes like a laser on Jaylin's pretty dick. Chase couldn't get enough of it. The fluttering of her eyes and constant lip biting said so. I couldn't get enough either, but I fast forwarded the video, shaking my head. My insides were sticky and I needed an ice-cold shower. I removed the flash drive and stuck it into my pocket. Afterward, I went to the bathroom and snatched off my clothes. The thought of cameras in the bathroom alarmed me, but then I remembered something Chase wrote in her letter. She mentioned that she put the camera in the bathroom before she woke up Jaylin, and removed it in the morning. I hoped so, but it really didn't matter. The only thing people would see was a horny-ass woman, playing with herself. As for the video of Chase, Roc, and Jaylin, I thought about putting that sucker on the internet or selling it to the tabloids to make money. Probably more money than I'd make by staying in this house. Nothing was set in stone yet, but it was surely an option.

Once my shower was over, I used the cell phone that Chase had provided and called her. She answered right away, but her voice was soft.

"Who is this?" she asked.

"Jada," I whispered into the phone. "I wanted to let you know that I got your package. I can't believe what you said in your letter. Is all of it really true?"

"Every bit of it. Roc is going down for this, and can you believe it? I had no idea, and I couldn't say anything until I got the facts. Now, I have all of the ammunition I need to win this challenge. In the process, I can seek a little revenge pertaining to my long, lost sister."

"I feel you on all of that, but you can't win this challenge without me. Don't get ahead of yourself."

"I'm not. I do understand how much I need you. You will benefit from this too, so let's not argue about things that in no way matter right now. I need to go take care of a few things, so we'll talk soon. Keep the phone on you at all times, but make sure the ringer is off. Did you get the flash drive?"

"Yes, I did. I looked at some of the video. Seeing y'all get down like that had me runnin' to the bathroom to cool down. I'm still in here, tryin' to regroup."

Chase laughed. "I'm still trying to recuperate myself, but it was fun. We'll talk more later, but for now, I must go."

We ended the call on that note. I sat for a moment, thinking if all of this would really work out. Then, I called my girl Portia to see what she'd been up to.

"What's up?" she yelled into the phone. "Where is the letter you were supposed to write me? Trice said you called her, and I feel real dissed."

My friends were so damn silly. I ignored Portia's comment about Trice. "I haven't had time to write, but it has been so wild and crazy up in here. I can't wait to tell you what's been goin' on, but you must tell me what's been happenin' over there first. Did Shay get that job at the bus station? And I know you got into Montel's shit for havin' that chick's phone number in his pocket."

"Girl, I beat that mofo's ass and tossed him out of here. He had the odyssey to tell me the number wasn't my bitness. Ain't that nothin'?"

"He should've known better to say that to you, especially since he ain't payin' no kinds of bills there. But I believe the word you were lookin' for was audacity, not odyssey. That didn't make no sense, and even I know that."

Portia ignored me. I rolled my eyes because she sounded like a damn fool. It made me think about my mispronunciation of words. I had to get better. That shit was embarrassing.

She went on and on about what had been going on while I was away. I barely got in one word, and every time I opened my mouth, she cut me off. I kept rolling my eyes and sighing. But after a while, I told her the battery was low and hung up. I then called the nappy-head li'l dude I considered my man. Kenny answered on the third ring.

"Where the fuck have you been? You must be hemmed up with another nigga somewhere. If you have been, you can stay with that muthafucka."

Maybe I was wrong for not telling Kenny where I was going, but he didn't seem to care anyway. And then for me to call and for him to diss me was totally uncalled for. I wasn't feeling his tone.

"Calm down, fool. All you know is I could've been locked up or adducted, I mean abducted, and you over there actin' a doggone fool. Tone yo voice down, Kenny, or else this conversation will be over."

"Bitch, I don't—"

I ended the call. I needed to rethink the folks I had in my circle. They were a hot-ass mess. It might take longer for me to disassociate myself from my troublesome girlfriends, but as for Kenny, I suspected that our relationship would soon be a wrap. With fine-ass men in the world like Jaylin and Roc, I was tripping by staying with Kenny. Then, the more I thought about it, Kenny had paid my rent for the last two months. Maybe, he was a keeper.

I had been in the bathroom for too long, so I hurried to leave. Making sure the coast was clear, I stuck my head out the door and looked from left to right. No one was there. I tiptoed back to the computer. I searched for media outlets that would be interested in buying the flash drive, hoping like hell that I had some luck.

Jaylin

When all was said and done, talked about and discussed over and over again, there was only one overall real winner in here. That was still me.

What Chase had done was, nonetheless, foul. But I wasn't the least bit tripping. There were doggy-dog men as well as women. She damn sure fit the bill, but many could say the same about me.

I kind of admired a woman who could be that cold. The problem with Chase was she still carried too much bitterness inside of her, resulting from the past. She was out for revenge, and whoever stood in her way to getting some kind of payback, they had to pay.

In no way did I lie to Roc when I told him Chase could be trouble. To be honest, I couldn't figure out anything that I'd said or done inside of this house that would knock anybody off their feet. I was just being me. All anybody in my circle had to do was ask me what went down in here and I would tell them the truth.

With that being said, it wasn't that easy for Roc. He seemed on edge since Chase had left, but we hadn't talked much about our time with her. I think Roc was worried about Desa Rae finding out some things. He was engaged to be married, but admitted that she hadn't set a wedding date. The whole situation seemed sticky. With Chase being out of the house, there was no telling what she was doing. Roc had some major concerns and he talked about them as we sat in the bedroom. We had just walked inside from playing a game of tennis.

"I hate to keep bringing this up, but Chase seems like she be on some slick shit. After what she did, you know I don't trust her to keep her mouth shut."

Worry was visible on Roc's face. He got up from the bed and paced the floor. Since he'd won the tennis game against me and Jada, he promised her that he'd have a cookie bake-off with her, if she'd stop pouting. Cooking was definitely something she thought she'd win at.

"I said this to you before, man, and must I repeat myself again. That is, if you're so worried, go home. It makes no sense for you to be that uptight and still be here."

"And like I said before, I'm no quitter. Whatever is waitin' for me at home will be there when I get there. I wish I could call to make sure everything is all good. I don't want no surprises, if you know what I mean."

I didn't bother to reply. Roc wasn't trying to hear what I was saying. He went into the closet, then came back out with clothes in his hands. "I need to wash some more of my clothes. They startin' to pile up on me."

"That's what happens when you're lazy."

He laughed, then headed toward the door. "I know what I meant to ask you," he said. "You already know that I'm a li'l irritated about this shit with Chase, right? It's left a bad taste in my mouth, not with you, but with her. But riddle me this. Why it ain't fuckin' with you like it is me? What if yo down chick gets word of what happened here?"

"Down chick, my ass. My down chick ain't down no more, she got fed up with the dumb shit. She hasn't been down for quite some time. Chase can do no harm to me whatsoever. You, my brotha, need to chill. If you were that worried about this getting back to Desa Rae, why you run up in another pussy?"

"I could ask myself the same question, but you know how we do it. On a for real tip, I talked myself into that shit. Smokin' all that weed contributed to my actions and the weed had me tryin' to justify my actions in my head."

"So, let me get this straight. It was the weed's fault. If what happened here does get back to Desa Rae, you'd better think of a better excuse than that. That won't fly. I'm just being real with you."

"I'm hopeful that it won't get back to her, but it's been on my mind more because of a silly-ass dream I had. But after today, I'mma let this go. I don't want to lose my baby over no bullshit with Chase, and I'm serious when I say I will hurt a bitch for tryin' to shake up things."

"Let's hope you don't have to. And on a final note, make sure you clean up your mess before you get married. Things from the past can come back to haunt. I'm a man who is telling you this from experience."

"I feel you. It's all good. The way I look at that is like this. We're not married yet, so I'm glad that this happened before I got married, not after. That will be my defense, if I have to use it. Most men have pre-weddin' day pussy, so you can't hold a nigga accountable for that."

Roc said nothing else and left the room. I couldn't help but to think how fucked he really was. There was no doubt that he had underestimated Chase.

I changed into shorts and a polo shirt. Before going into the kitchen with Jada and Roc, I straightened my side of the closet and sprayed Lysol in it. With three people already gone, the closet wasn't that crowded anymore. It was still junky, though.

Noticing a pair of Jada's jeans dropped over her shoes, I picked them up to fold them. I hated for people not to take care of their clothes. If hangers were in the closet, why not use them? Inside of her jeans was a pair of silk, light purple panties. I frowned as soon as I noticed pussy juice stains in the middle of the crotch. Something definitely had her hot and bothered. I shook the panties from her jeans and they fell on the floor. So did a flash drive that I picked up and held in my hand. I kicked the panties aside, and then placed her jeans on a hanger. Afterward, I put the flash drive in my pocket to see what was on it later.

Roc and Jada had the kitchen in one big mess. Bowls, flour, cracked eggs, milk, butter, sugar—you name it, it was there.

"What took you so long?" Roc asked. "I need some help with this. You know anything about makin' cookies?"

"No doubt. I have one of the best cooks in the world living with me. We call her Nanny B, and she taught me everything that *you* need to know about cooking."

Jada already had her lips pursed. "Just so you know, we ain't interested in fat-free cookies. If you're goin' to help, be sure to add sugar, butter, and cookin' oil to the mix. After that, you can experiment with whatever you'd like to and go from there."

"It doesn't take all of that to make cookies. Where are the big bowls at? I need to show you something and then maybe you'll shut your mouth."

"FYI," Roc said. "Find your own bowl, because I like my cookies sweet. Real sweet and smoky."

Roc reached for his bag of weed and had the nerve to sprinkle his cookie dough with marijuana.

"Yeah, buddy." Jada happily slapped his back. "Add a li'l bit more of that, baby. It seems like you know what'cha doin'."

Roc added more. I just shook my head. They couldn't have been serious about this cookie cook-off. If so, I reminded myself not to sample any of Roc's cookies.

I put my game face on and gathered a few bananas, some oatmeal, dates and raisins, vegetable oil, and vanilla extract. No sugar, no butter. I reached for a bowl and some measuring cups, then took my items over to the kitchen table. As I started to measure my ingredients, Jada came over to mess with me.

"Why you over here tryin' to look like you know what you doin'?" she asked.

"Because I do know what I'm doing. Now, back up, you're in my space. You're too close and you're breath is hot."

Jada bumped her hip with mine, almost knocking me aside. "All I gotta say is those cookies better be good or else I'm gon' drive you nonstop. You need to add some sugar and butter to your batch, because things are already lookin' mighty dry."

I ignored Jada, but she kept coming back over to the table, hovering over me and my batter. She couldn't deny that things were looking up for me, especially when I put the dough on a cookie sheet and got ready to pop them in the oven.

"They do look a lot better than Roc's cookies do." She tried to whisper, but he heard her.

"Looks can be deceivin,' as we all now know. Wait until my cookies are done until you pass any kind of judgment on them."

Into the oven his cookies went. Jada followed with her third tray of cookies. She thought she was so good that she had to make three different kinds.

We stood around in the kitchen, talking and waiting patiently for the cookies to get done.

"Please tell me why men are so competitive," Jada said. "I blew the tennis game earlier because I'm so tired of y'all tryin' to compete against each other. What's with that?"

I responded before Roc had a chance to. "No, you blew the game earlier because you don't know how to play. As for men, we have a competitive nature. It is what it will always be and nothing will ever change. We strive to win and don't like it when we lose."

"Nope, losin' ain't a good feelin'," Roc said. "But, hey, somebody always has to lose. It won't be me on this cookie challenge, and no offense, but y'all time here will be cut short."

Jada rolled her neck around. "I disagree, but keep yo unrealistic hopes alive. Ain't nothin' wrong with competin' with each other, but, uh, do y'all like to compete for women? Mainly, what about this whole thing with Chase? I'm not bein' nosy, but were y'all competin' for her?"

I started not to touch this, only because my words would offend Roc. The way I saw it, when it came to women, there was no comparison between us. Therefore, there was no need to compete with a man who wasn't on my level. I was glad when Roc opened his mouth first.

"Ma, there wasn't no competition between Jaylin and me. And competin' with any man over a woman is not somethin' that I do. Chase had a motive and she followed her agenda. Her desire was to get some dick and she got it. She had been sweatin' a nigga from day one. The money was never her priority."

Jada rubbed her chin. "So, you believe that all Chase wanted out of this was dick? I guess that could've been the case, but how do you feel that she not only got yo dick, but Jaylin's dick too? In the same day, and only hours apart. That has to sting, doesn't it?"

"First of all," I said. "If y'all believe the only motive Chase had was dick, you're fooling yourselves. I can't put my finger on her motive yet, but believe me when I say there was more to it. Secondly, who gives a damn how much dick she got? It ain't like me or Roc running around here, trying to take that shit back. No matter how you look at it, I had a good time. My dick was satisfied and she left here with an elated pussy."

Roc gave me dap, but Jada continued to push.

"But in a sense, you did get Roc's leftovers. And then he's left feelin' like all he did wasn't enough to satisfy her. That must be fuckin' with y'all heads, ain't it?"

"No," we said in unison. Roc added more. It was obvious that we both felt frustrated by Jada's view of things. "You talkin' about leftovers. Really? Truth is, we all bein' served leftovers. When you go behind the next muthafucka, that's just how it is. All I'm gon' say to you is I did my part—well. If Chase was still horny after how I put it out there, that's on her, not me."

"I know, 'cause you did go over and above the call of duty."

I had to ask Jada a question. "How do you know what that man did? Were you watching?"

"No, I wasn't watchin'. Chase told me some things before she left. Things that neither of you will ever know. It's our secret."

See, she was fucking with us, but I wasn't biting. Neither was Roc. He went over to the stove and removed our cookies from the oven.

"Jada, it looks like your cookies need another minute or two. I'm leavin' yours in there."

"Let me see," she said, rushing over to the oven. "You may be tryin' to let my cookies burn."

After looking in the oven, she agreed that a few more minutes were needed. I waited for my cookies to cool before putting them on a plate. Roc did the same. By the time he finished, Jada's cookies were done.

She was singing and dancing all around the kitchen, knowing that she was the winner, based on looks. Truth be told, Roc's cookies looked like mountains of shit. Mine weren't too bad, but the oats had gotten a little browner than I had expected.

Jada carefully placed all of her cookies on a plate and introduced her display.

"These here are my famous sugar cookies, these are my very chocolatey-chocolate cookies, and these are my peanut butter with extra nuts cookies. Roc, you go first, baby. Only because I know Jaylin is goin' to find somethin' to complain about. Please enjoy."

Roc picked up the chocolate cookie, chewed then nodded. He bit into the sugar cookie, then the peanut butter one. Right after he swallowed, he leaned over and kissed Jada on her cheek.

"You have an investor and we sellin' those cookies as soon as we get back on our turf. The peanut butter ones are the best, but they definitely all good."

"Thank you, Chef Roc," Jada said with glee in her eyes. "But I'm the only person who makes money off my skills. Sorry."

He laughed, then tasted my cookie. I waited for his response with a slight grin on my face. He chewed and chewed some more. Then he opened his mouth and cleared his throat.

"Not bad, but not good either. I needed more flava, so I'm on the fence."

Jada giggled and all I could say was, "Whatever."

It was my turn, so I took tiny bites from Jada's three cookies and washed them down with cold water.

"There is no such word as chocolately-chocolate, and all I tasted was a bunch of sugar and dough. Your investment wouldn't be worth it, Roc, don't waste your time."

Surprisingly, all Jada did was give me the finger. Roc waited for me to taste his cookie, but I wasn't touching it.

"Nigga, I ate yours, didn't I?" he said with a frown. "Fair is fair, ain't it?"

"I don't always play fair, but since you about to cry about it, I guess a tiny bite won't hurt."

He also gave me the finger.

I picked up the cookie, sniffing it. It didn't smell too bad, so I bit into it and chewed. Awful. But just to mess with Jada, I took another bite. "Now, this right here is pretty good. I got my money on Roc."

Roc laughed, but Jada got mad. "Get the hell out of here. You know darn well that his cookie ain't better than mine."

"Hey, in my opinion it is. You can't offer your opinion if you haven't tasted it."

Jada snatched one of his cookies from the plate. She bit into it, then spat the chewed up cookie in her hand. "Are you kiddin' me?" she shouted. "That cookie is terrible. It don't even taste like a cookie."

"You mad because my cookie tastes better than yours. Stop hatin,' ma. It's not a good look."

Jada threw her hand back and tasted my cookie. This time, she ran to the sink to spit it out and rinsed her mouth. "Yucky," she said with a twisted face. "What was that?"

"It's called the best cookie you ever ate. Forget what you talking about, baby. It's time to choose a winner. Like I said before, I got my money on Roc."

Roc pointed to his chest. "I got my money on me too, so with two votes out of three, I won."

Like always, Jada got mad and pouted. "I should've known that y'all wouldn't play fair and would stick together. Don't ask me to do nothin' else with y'all. I'm done."

She stormed off, but all I did was laugh and shrug. Roc and I started to clean the kitchen. By the time we finished, it was almost five o'clock. Roc said that he was going to chill outside and listen to some music by the pool. I told him I'd be out later because I wanted to get some washing done.

I entered the bedroom, and when I entered the closet, I noticed that Jada was in a panic, looking for something.

"What are you looking for?" I asked.

For whatever reason, she was fidgeting. "No...nothin'. I'm straightenin' some of my things."

The one thing that I could tell was when I was being lied to, especially by a woman. Jada hadn't straightened anything and her clothes were the exact same way as they were before. It was obvious that she was looking for the flash drive, because she kept checking her jean pockets.

She made me more curious about what was on the drive, but I couldn't help but to mess with her about the cookies.

"Say, about the cookie thing. Truth is, your cookies were hooked up. They were good, but if you cut the sugar in half, they'd be better."

All she did was display a fake smile. I was surprised that she didn't give me any more gripe. Her eyes were still searching through her clothes in the closet. She then stepped out of it.

"Oh, well," she said with a sigh. "Roc promised that he would show me some swimmin' techniques, so I'm goin' outside. What else you gon' do?"

"I'm gon' wash some of my clothes. Then I'll be outside to go for a swim and finish up the book I'm reading. Don't drown before I get there."

Jada chuckled, and after tossing her swimming suit over her shoulder, she left the room. I kept my eyes on her. The first place she went was to the computer desk. She looked around, picked up some papers on the desk, then checked the back of the computer. She put her hands on her hips, then sighed again.

Afterward, she went to the bathroom to change. I waited until she left the bathroom and went outside. That was when I went to the computer and stuck the flash drive in it.

The first thing I saw was Chase and Roc having sex in the living room. I wanted to back away from the computer, but couldn't. How or why in the hell did Jada have this in her possession? I didn't know. But no matter what, it was very damaging to Roc. He wasn't playing with the pussy, and the way Chase conducted herself with him was not the way she was with me. Maybe it was done on purpose. I had a feeling that she wanted Roc to be seen as the aggressive one, and her as the passive one. It surely appeared that way, and it was almost like she knew she was being taped. Poor Roc hadn't a clue. If Desa Rae ever got a hold of this, he would find himself doing serious damage control. I was anxious to tell him about the flash drive. I knew it was going to cause him to lose it. He'd already been uptight, but this would surely send him over the edge.

I hit the fast-forward button to see what else was on the flash drive. I guess I shouldn't have been surprised to see Chase and me in action. We were getting it in. The video showed everything that had transpired into the wee hours of the morning. I wasn't in the same predicament as Roc was with Desa Rae finding out about this, but it wasn't like I wasn't concerned about something like this getting into the wrong hands. Being in Jada's hands was enough, and to invade my privacy like this wasn't cool.

No matter what, I had to get at Jada and figure out her purpose for having the flash drive, without her knowing that I'd removed it from her jeans. It was apparent that Chase was in on this shit too, but to what extent? Was she trying to get at Roc, me, or both of us? Jada and Chase had definitely barked up the wrong tree, and what a mess they had made.

As I was in deep thought, I heard someone walking down the hallway. Not knowing who it was, I hurried to remove the flash drive, easing it into my pocket. Right after that, I saw Jeff.

"What's up, Jaylin?" he asked, as if he already knew what was up. "Did I catch you at a bad time?"

I played clueless. "Not at all. I was checking out a few things on the internet, and decided to reply to some of my fan mail. I tend to get a lot of it and can barely keep up."

He nodded, then put his hands into his pockets. "That's because so many people love you or hate to love you. They seem curious about you, and that's a good thing, isn't it?"

"Most definitely. Can't say that you'll ever hear me complaining."

"Good. But here's the deal. I told you that I'd be back with my decision, so I'm here to have a discussion with you. After further investigation, I determined that you did break the rules by open- ing the door to let your ex-girlfriend inside. However, I don't think it's my duty to remove you from this house."

There was a small sigh of relief from me, but there also wasn't a chance in hell that I'd let Jeff put me out of this house. Ex- girlfriend, my ass.

"But, Jaylin, I think, to be fair, that we should tell Jada and Roc about this. If they think you should go, then I'm afraid that you'll have to leave."

I stared at Jeff, wanting to punch him in his face. But in an effort to put this incident behind me, I was down for what he had sug- gested. Once this was over with, I couldn't wait to confront Jada about the flash drive. I figured what was on the video would concern Roc, and he definitely needed to know there was some trickery shit going on around here. I had a good feeling about who was behind it.

Jeff went outside to get Jada and Roc. I sat on the couch, watching as they came inside laughing and dripping wet from being in the pool. Roc wiped down his face with a towel, then tossed it over to Jada so she could dry off.

"Man," Roc said, making his way into the living room. He seemed almost out of breath. "This chick is crazy. She almost drowned my ass."

"I did not. You're the one who told me to stand on your shoulders while you were underwater."

"Why would I tell you to do that? What I said was stand back so I could free my shoulders."

Jeff interjected. "Thankfully, no one was hurt. Sounds like there was a simple mix-up between the two of you. But have a seat and let me explain a certain mix-up we seem to have in this house."

I stroked my goatee with a tad bit of anger trapped in my eyes. "There ain't no mix-up. You're only confused by what actually happened and you don't have your facts together."

"Maybe so. That's why I'm giving Jada and Roc an opportunity to clear this up. Afterward, we can move on."

Roc and Jada took their seats and listened to Jeff explain his side of what had happened. I had already spoken to Roc about everything. The plan was for us to stick together, no matter what. But this was new to Jada. She didn't seem interested in what Jeff was saying and neither did Roc. He kept shrugging as Jeff kept putting emphasis on me breaking the rules.

"So, to sum it up," he said. "I want the two of you to decide if Jaylin should have to leave this house or not. It has to be a unanimous decision or else he stays."

This could turn out simple, especially since I saved Jada from leaving when she got into it with Prince. The question was would she do the same for me?

Roc and Jada turned in my direction. I put my arms on top of the couch and crossed one of my legs over the other. This was about to get real interesting, especially since I knew what I had in my pocket—the flash drive.

"When do we have to decide?" Jada asked Jeff. "Now?"

He nodded. "Yes, as in right now. Ladies first."

Jada's mouth dropped open. "Here we go with this mess again. Why I gotta be the one to go first? Why not Roc?"

"Because he told you to make the call first," Roc said to her. He glanced over at me, giving me a slow nod, as if he had my back.

Jada made a ticking sound with her mouth. She searched me from head to toe while scratching her head.

"Dang, Jaylin, I don't know what to do. I hate to be put into a preditment like this, and we have had so much fun around here, haven't we?"

"A lot of fun, and we've learned some valuable things that we need to apply to our everyday lives. With that being said, the word is predicament, not preditment."

"Thank you for that tad bit of information, but at a time like this, I preferred for you not to go there. Boo, I know you think my decision shouldn't be hard, but it is. While you know I ain't got nothin' but love for you, this is a challenge that I really and truly want to win. As only you know, we got this li'l thing goin' on between us and I'm not sure if you gon' follow through." She paused and continued in thought. I assumed she was thinking about the money I had offered to her. She could forget it if she made the decision to vote me out over some bullshit.

"Okay," she said, smacking. "What I'm hopin' is that you're a man of your word like you say you are. And that you'll be happy for me, if I win." She paused to touch her chest. "With all of that bein' said, my dear, sweet, loveable friend, I've enjoyed your company soooo much. I don't know what I'mma do without you around here, but you did break the rules. Therefore, you need to go pack yo bags and get yo highly educated self out of here."

I almost couldn't believe Jada's decision, but then again, yes I could. I said not one word. Nothing but a crisp silence soaked the room. I looked over Jada's shoulder at Roc. The ball was in his court. He damn sure better had known how to play it. If not, he was going to be fucked!

BOOK CLUB QUESTIONS

1. After reading *Hell House Part Two*, who do you now believe will be the winner?

2. Do you think Sylvia should have been the first person voted out of the house? Why or why not?

3. Would you come up with a plot to win this challenge or would you play fair and square. Share your plot to win or what would you do to get the other participants out of the house?

4. Do you think Jaylin should have to leave the house for inviting Brashaney to come inside? Why or why not?

5. Roc and Desa Rae are from the Full Figured Series. How do you feel about older women dating younger men?

6. Chase is known for being scandalous. How do you feel about women having sex with multiple men, versus men having sex with multiple women? Should there be different standards?

7. Sylvia fell in love with her best friend's husband. Do you believe that people can control who they fall in love with? Why or why not?

8. The participants in Hell House have one bathroom, they're limited on the computer, they have one TV, and have no access to cell phones. If you were inside of this house, what would be the hardest thing for you to do without?

9. The fight between Jada and Prince got out of hand. We all know that Jada put her hands on Prince first, but do you believe that her actions justified what Prince did to her?

AUTHOR'S NOTE

I'm eager to hear from you! Please visit hellhouse.homestead. com to send comments regarding your Hell House experience. If you would like to ask questions or send "fan mail" to any of the characters, and possibly have your inquiry answered in the next book, please follow the submissions guidelines.

READING JUST GOT MORE FUN!
Naughty 1
Naughty 2
Naughty 3
Naughty 4: Naughty by Nature
Naughty 5: Too Naughty
Naughty No More
Jaylin's World: Dare to live in it!

Full Figured 1
Full Figured 3
Full Figured 5
Who Ya Wit (Full Figured Finale)

How Can I Be Down?
No Justice No Peace

ABOUT THE AUTHOR

A St. Louis native, Brenda Hampton is recognized for being a writer who brings the heat. She has written over twenty-plus novels, including anthologies, and her literary career is filled with many accomplishments. Her name has graced the *Essence* magazine bestsellers list, and she was named a favorite female fiction writer in *Upscale* magazine. Her mystery novel, *The Dirty Truth*, was nominated for an African American Literary Award, and she was awarded, by Infini Promotions, for being the best female writer.

Hampton's dedication to her career, and her original literary works, led to a multibook deal. She works as a literary representative for an array of talented authors, and she is the executive producer of an upcoming reality TV show, based out of St. Louis, Missouri where she resides.

In an effort to show appreciation to her colleagues in literature, Hampton created The Brenda Hampton Honorary Literacy Award and Scholarship Fund. The award not only celebrates writers, but it also represents unique individuals who put forth every effort to uphold the standards of African-American literature. Visit the author at www.brendamhampton.com and www.hellhouse.homestead.com.

I couldn't believe that I agreed to do this bullshit. And it surprised me when I stepped inside of the so-called Hell House in St. Louis and didn't see anyone. The *Miami Vice*-style glass doors left me with a dramatic first impression that was kind of dope. I could very well be satisfied living here for the next three months; the living conditions resembled a penthouse I used to have while selling cocaine. That was then, this is now. Now, I was on lock by my fiancée, Desa Rae Jenkins, who recently suggested that we needed to explore life and try different things. In other words, she was tired of my black ass hanging around

her house and wanted a break from our relationship. I also needed a break, so I jumped on this opportunity to jet away for a while.

I dropped my Nike duffle bag at the door and glanced upwards at the vaulted, sloped ceiling. The smell of newness was in the air and the glossy marble floor in the foyer was polished to perfection, displaying a glare of my chocolate fineness. *Umph*, I thought while staring at the blurred image of me. I wet my thick lips, then headed toward the kitchen to scope the rest of the amenities in this immaculate one-story crib.

"What up? Anybody here?" I called out, cautiously taking slow steps down a narrow hallway that had framed pictures of modern art on the freshly painted white walls. My new Air Jordans left imprints in the cottony carpet that led to a spacious, sunken living room area on the right and an urban-style kitchen with stainless steel appliances to the left. Checking out my surroundings, I narrowed my eyes into the living room that was laid out with a horseshoe-shaped microfiber sofa and square pillows. A forty-two-inch flat-screen TV was mounted on the wall. Underneath the TV were bookshelves filled with many books for someone's reading pleasure—definitely not mine. Numerous multicolored beanbags were also in the living room, and I assumed they were there for chilling purposes.

The living room could be chalked up as simple, but the high-priced kitchen was kicking ass. Everything was white, navy or stainless steel. Navy pendant lights hung above a white rectangular countertop that was surrounded with wavy curved-back barstools that had a steel finish. The decorator damn sure needed a kiss, but she wouldn't get one from me since I was now a reformed man.

While thinking about Desa Rae, I eased my hands into my jean pockets and looked out a sliding glass door that viewed a backyard my hood relatives could only dream of. There was an Olympic-sized swimming pool with crystal-clear blue water, tennis and basketball courts, and rock waterfalls used for diving. The lawn was well manicured and lounge chairs were all over the patio. At 103 degrees outside, I damn sure knew where most of my time would be spent. Yeah, my skin color was already black as charcoal, so I wasn't worried about the sun baking it much more.

I was getting impatient and sighed after licking my lips again. The motherfuckers running this show told me to be here at two o'clock, but when I looked at my watch, it was already two-thirty. Deciding to see what else was up, I turned away from the kitchen to go check out where I would have to lay my head. I noticed that the carpet trail split into two directions, so I shifted to the left first, entering a modern bathroom with unique stainless steel faucets, a pearly white toilet and a shower squared with thick glass. All the white made me nervous. I sure as hell hoped that I wouldn't be shacked up in this crib with a bunch of nasty people. I was eager to see who those people would be, especially the women—for whatever reason that might be.

I backtracked to the other hallway and that was where I found a room with three full-sized beds against one wall and three beds against the wall in front of it. The beds were covered with multicolored comforters and colorful sheets. Wasn't feeling that shit and the beds were too small. Nametags with our names on them sat near the edge of each bed. One by one I checked out the names, noticing that the brothers were on one side of the room and the sisters were on the other. That didn't work for me either, so I rearranged some things. I put my nametag on the bed that was in between Chase's and Sylvia's beds. Jada's nametag I put between Prince's and Jaylin's beds. I hoped Jada wasn't the finest one in the bunch, but then again it didn't matter either way. I was on lock. That was today, didn't account for tomorrow.

There was no window in the cramped room, but there was one sizeable walk-in closet. It was obvious that all this room was good for was sleeping and fucking. Didn't think I'd be spending much time chilling in the bedroom, so I made my exit, realizing that time was moving on and my grand tour of this crib was over.

I took another look at my watch, then reached into my pocket to grab my cell phone. Somebody needed to tell me what the fuck was up. I was getting impatient. A nigga like me was beginning to think this was some kind of setup. I'd been in these situations before. My instincts were saying run! The information guide and itinerary that I received said the meet and greet of contestants would begin at two. It was way after two, so fuck it. I felt the need to jet, so I put my phone back into my pocket and grabbed my duffle bag. Once it was on my shoulder, I headed toward the door, but was stopped dead in my tracks when I saw a taxi pull up. I squinted as I peeked through the glass, trying to get a glimpse at the fine-ass woman whose peep-toe stilettos had touched the ground. She had long, light-skinned legs that were made for riding. I was eager to see her face, and as soon as she exited the taxi, I could feel my nature trying to rise. That ass was fat and those hips swayed with rhythm as she made her way up the long driveway. Her weaved-in ponytail swung from side to side and was tightly pulled back, making her hazel eyes slant. I sucked in a deep breath and backed away from the door. Checked myself again, while looking down at the floor and hoping that the white wife-beater I had on wasn't too laid-back. It showed my tats that so many women loved and I figured she wouldn't be able to look away from my bulging muscles. Lance Gross didn't have shit on me, but there were some who would beg to differ. This chick, however, was classy and I liked that. She wasn't *Full Figured* how I normally liked my women, but I could definitely work with her. Unfortunately, if this was Jada, I had already messed up by putting her nametag on the other side of the room. Big mistake, no doubt, but after this bullshit was over I was sure there would be plenty.

Chase

I saw his blackness through the door, but why wouldn't he come outside to help me with my bags? Some men were so lazy and he obviously wasn't the exception. I hoped that someone else was here to help me. I had about six bags in the taxi and needed some assistance. The taxi driver claimed that he had broken his leg, but my question to him was where were the crutches? He didn't have an answer for that and I didn't have an answer for my wallet somehow disappearing. That is what I planned to tell him, once I got my belongings out of his taxi.

Instead of pushing on the front door, I pursed my lips and knocked with an attitude. It was scorching hot outside, and I was dying for a glass of ice-cold water. But when the door flew open, my thirst was more than quenched by saliva that almost slipped from my wide mouth. The rule was to never let a man see me sweat, so I quickly clamped my mouth shut, trying to downplay my instant attraction to the brother on the other side of the door. With tattoos running up and down his arms, he looked to be straight out of prison. But so damn what! I loved a man who was a bit rough around the edges, and I'd had enough of the business- minded married ones with clingy wives who liked to start trouble. After seeing him, my whole attitude had changed. I almost broke a heel as I rushed inside to see if he had been invited to Hell House, too. Right now, it felt more like Heaven's House.

I held out my hand to shake his. "And you are?" I said, awaiting an answer.

"Yo baby daddy." He smiled, displaying those snow-white teeth against all that black. Lord have mercy on me. I couldn't help but to play along with him.

"Well, baby daddy, do you think you can help me with my bags? They're still out in the taxi. The driver claims that his leg is broken and he won't help me."

"I got you," he said, passing by me to go outside. His good-smelling cologne tickled my nose and left me standing in awe. I was in a daze until I heard his voice. It shook me from my thoughts.

"Wha…what did you say?" I said, watching as he walked backward down the driveway.

"I said, since I got you, you gotta have me, too. That's on a for real tip right there."

Okay, so his language wasn't all that great, but I still gave him a nod. If this worked out, yeah, I had his back, front, side and then some. I was single, loving it and hadn't made any commitments to anyone, especially since that trick, Liz, caught me in bed with her husband. Liz was my boss and that day still haunts me. I've been careful not to date married men with bright wives. If she wasn't bright then that was a different story. The hubby was considered fair game and nine times out of ten he was mine.

My baby daddy was trying to impress me by carrying all six bags into the house. A sheen of sweat covered his forehead and he pulled up his wife-beater to dab the sweat. I got a glimpse of his abs. The look of them almost sent me to my knees, begging him to slip something into my mouth. I wanted to rip his clothes off right then and there, but I didn't want to blow it, as I had done so many times in the past.

"Thank you so much, but please tell me your name," I said.

"Roc," he said. How fitting for a stallion of a man like him? "But before you tell me yo name, you'd better go outside to pay the taxi driver. He's about to clown on yo ass. I wouldn't want him to do that, especially since I'm enjoyin' the look of it."

I didn't respond, but since he was enjoying *it*, I made sure he got a good look at my butt as I sashayed back to the taxi. I could only imagine what Roc was thinking. My tight, gray skirt hugged my backside like a long lost best friend, and my red silk shirt was draped low in the front, showing off my 36 C's. I had no idea what I was going to embark upon coming to Hell House, but I was thankful that my attire was professional and sexy.

"How much do I owe you?" I inquired to the taxi driver while digging into my purse.

The Fred Sanford-looking black man cut his eyes at me and then he pointed to his meter. "The car was still runnin' while you were inside. You owe me a hundred and fifty-two dollars."

It sounded like he had gunpowder clogged in his throat. My hand quickly moved to my hip and the attitude was back.

"One hundred and fifty what?" I yelled. "Are you kidding me?"

He had the audacity to put up his hand, displaying the numbers. "Five. Two. Fifty-two and the meter is still runnin'."

"And I'm going to be running in a minute as well because that is too much money. Besides, I can't seem to find my wallet. Did I leave it on the backseat?"

Yep, he was playing me like a fool, but please *Don't Even Go There* because I could play him so much better. I opened the back door and bent over to feel the floor, as if I was searching for my wallet. Roc was getting a clear view of what to expect when he hit it from the back, and without any panties on, I bent further over.

"I don't know what happened to my wallet. Are you sure you didn't see it?" I said to the driver.

"No, I didn't see yo wallet, but you need to get my money or else there's about to be some trouble."

See, he just pissed me off. Some men hadn't a clue where to draw the line. Was he really going to beat my ass because I didn't have the money? No. I eased out of the backseat and closed the door.

"Unfortunately, I can't find my wallet," I said with a shrug. "Either you can call the police or overcharge some of your other customers to make up the difference."

"Or, I can get out of this taxi and fuck you up. That's what I'm about to do!"

He swung the door open and hopped out of the taxi like he was trained by Bruce Lee. Broken leg, my ass. I didn't have to say one word because my baby daddy was right there to intervene.

"What's up, old school?" Roc asked as he stood over the taxi driver in a very intimidating manner. "Why you out here tryin' to rip this woman off? You didn't even want to help her with her bags, and now you disrespectin' her over some money? She said she lost her wallet, so nothin' else needs to be said."

The taxi driver backed away from Roc, but I stood close behind him in case something popped off. If anyone was going to get cut, it wasn't going to be me. Baby daddy was going down by himself.

"Look, man, just get this broad to give me my money. After that I'm out of here. If not, I'm gon' have to call the police. If I have to go that route, things will get ugly."

Maybe so because baby daddy looked like the kind of brother who probably had warrants. I didn't want him to get arrested, so I tried to compromise with the foolish taxi driver by offering him twenty dollars. "Here," I said, handing the bill to him. "It's all I have. Take it or leave it."

He reached inside of the taxi for his phone. "Fuck this shit. I should've called the police from the get-go."

"Dialin' the police means some blood may have to be shed," Roc said. "So think before you act. I don't have any dollars on me right now, but give me yo address and I'll mail the rest to you later."

It was obvious that Roc was gangsta, but there was no need for blood to shed. The old man pondered what to do and then all of our eyes shifted to a triple-black Mercedes with tinted windows. We could barely see who was inside, but when the passenger-side door swung open, I staggered backward and almost fell on my ass. Baby daddy had a twisted look on his face and the taxi driver stared as if he wished he were a woman. Almost in slow motion, a light-skinned brother with dark shades shielding his eyes emerged from the car. The smell of money was blowing through the air and we all inhaled it. He knew he was the shit and the ones who never smiled always had a big ego. I surely wanted to ignore him, but couldn't. He threw up the deuces sign to the driver and the driver backed away to leave. Professionally dressed like I was, the tailored navy suit he wore couldn't be duplicated. It had to be made specifically for him and the way it clung to the frame of his body was breathtaking. From the tip of the natural curls in his hair, to those shiny, black shoes that hit the pavement as he swaggered forward, he was flawless.

"I hope I'm not too late," he said, looking directly at me behind his stare. He was still at a short distance, but I was speechless, until baby daddy cleared his throat.

"Too late for what?" Roc asked. "Ain't too much of nothin' happenin' yet."

Shiiiit, baby daddy needed to speak for himself. There were a whole lot of things happening—inside of my coochie, of course. I was too ashamed to elaborate.

As Mr. Handsome came closer, he moved like a theme of music played in his head. His eyes gave me an intense stare down, and when he pulled his shades away from his face, I felt like his addictive steel-gray eyes were firing bullets from an AK-47. His gaze was so powerful that it sent shockwaves throughout my entire body. Sadly, I could feel a slow drip of sweat sliding down my forehead. *Get it together, Chase, now! Never let a man see you sweat or else you're screwed!* Right about now, getting screwed wasn't a bad idea.

"Nothing happening," Mr. Sexy said to me, ignoring Roc altogether. They both were checking me out and that was a good thing. "If ain't nothing happening, why is everybody outside looking irate?"

The taxi driver couldn't wait to speak up. "I dropped her off at this house, and she left me out here, sittin' in the car for at least thirty minutes. When she came back, I told her that she had to pay up. She got mad, and the next thing I know, this man out here yellin' and threatenin' to hurt me for only doin' my job. I don't want no trouble from nobody, but this cheap bitch done tried to get over on me. If she don't pay up, I will call the police."

"First of all," Roc said, preparing his defense for me. "Get yo time straight because she wasn't inside for no thirty minutes. If you had not lied to her about your leg bein' broken, this wouldn't even be no problem. Fess up and admit to your laziness. I wouldn't pay you one damn dime either, so why don't you go ahead and call the police?"

I surely didn't want the cab driver to do that, only because the police might force me to pay the money. I hurried to speak up and was thrilled that Roc had already tried to make my case. "There's no need to call the police, but you need to cut what I owe you in half. Roc is right. I wasn't inside for thirty minutes and you're the one who is trying to get over."

The cab driver wasn't trying to hear what we were saying. He kept going on and on, and he even called me another bitch. I was about ready to let him have it, but then Mr. Handsome spoke up for me.

"Naw, she ain't no cheap bitch," the sexy man answered in my defense. "She too fine to fit into that category. But I agree—somebody definitely needs to pay you your money."

"That's all I'm sayin'," the taxi driver said, mean-mugging me.

Next thing I knew, Mr. Handsome reached into his pocket and pulled out a wad of cash that was barely secured with a diamond money holder. He flipped through three hundred dollars and gave it to the taxi driver.

"Problem solved," he replied to the driver. "Now jet before you catch a beat-down from this beautiful woman you done pissed off, or from thug lovin' who I know wouldn't mind putting his foot in your ass."

"All day, every day, especially when I feel a muthafucka is out of line," baby daddy shot back. But his comment was directed at the really cute one. All he did, though, was snicker and smooth walk his way toward the front door.

"Preciate you, bruh!" the driver shouted. "You are my kind of nigga!"

Mr. Sexy turned around, giving his head a slight tilt. He stroked his goatee and his eyes looked to be shooting real bullets at the driver who had obviously said the wrong thing. "My name is Jaylin Rogers. I don't go by no other name and calling me anything else will get you disrespected. You've been warned."

Well damn! I hoped he wouldn't be that upset when I referred to him as my baby daddy. At this point, I was confused about who I wanted to proudly wear that title. The driver threw his hand back and rushed back into the taxi. He sped off in a hurry. All I could think about was rewarding both of these handsome men for all that they'd done for me already. While observing Roc's backside as he walked in front of me, I was so sure I would be able to come up with something spectacular for my new room/playmates.

Jaylin

She was sexy and pretty—check. Nails done—check. Smelled good—check. Hair in order—check. Nice ass—check. No panty line—double check. Seems as if the only thing that concerned me was the status of her financial situation. I bet any amount of money that her credit score was fucked up. If she couldn't afford to pay the taxi driver, there wasn't no telling what else she couldn't afford.

In addition to that, the last thing I needed was to add another woman to my payroll. The ex-wife and ex-mistress were already milking me dry. Everybody had their hands out for something, and with all the cash I'd been dishing out, there was no way possible for me to retire again. I had to keep money flowing. As hard as I worked, there wasn't a chance in hell that I'd turn down a vacation or an opportunity like this one to get away. Three months sounded like a plan to me, but I had to check this place out to make sure I was down with it. If everything appeared to be in order, then I planned to call my best friend, Shane, and have him come back here to drop off my things. For now, though, my shit stayed in his car, until I felt comfortable with my surroundings.

For starters, the place was cool. It was nowhere near what I was used to, but what the hell? I liked white accessories, and from what I had seen about the house thus far, it looked spotless. I was digging the swimming pool, and when I stepped outside onto the patio, I noticed a nice-size workout area where I could exercise in the morning. There was also a game room with a pool table and bar. The bathroom, however, was a bit on the tiny side. As I looked at it, I realized how much I would probably miss my Jacuzzi. I closed the door and then made my way into what was supposed to be a bedroom. I was shocked to see how narrow and confined it was. It would take at least three of these beds to match mine, and what the fuck was up with the nametags and colorful décor covering the mattresses? I sat on one of the beds, making sure it was comfortable enough for me to sleep. It wasn't. I started to rethink the whole thing, but as I was in deep thought, I heard the door squeak open. In walked the woman who had snubbed the cab driver.

"Hello," she said with a bright smile. She took a seat on the bed in front of me, crossing her well-moisturized legs. "I see you checking out this house, huh? I am, too, but I wanted to thank you for paying the taxi driver for me. He was so rude to me; therefore, I felt no need to give him one dime."

I was trying to get a good read on this woman, so I didn't say much. I let her do most of the talking, yet kept my responses brief. "There's not much in here to check out, especially in this room."

She looked around, paying extra attention to the nametags. "So, whoever Jada is, she's supposed to sleep between you and Prince. As for me, my name is Chase and I'm to the left of Roc. He's the other nice-looking man out there, but I don't like to be the closest person to the door. Do you mind if I switch Jada's nametag with mine?"

I shrugged as if it didn't matter to me either way. It didn't. Chase switched the nametags and then she sat back on the bed directly across from me. She opened her legs wide, before crossing them again. My eyes shifted so quickly that I was sure she hadn't picked up on where they had flashed to. I saw her shaved pussy, and I hated for a woman to play games and tease me. Her actions reminded me too much of my children's mother, Scorpio. Strike one.

"So, you never told me," she said. "What do you think of this house? Can you see yourself staying here for three months with complete strangers?"

I sat back on my elbows and looked up at the cheap ceiling fan squeaking, as it turned in circles. "Maybe. Maybe not."

"What would be your reason for not staying?"

I shrugged. "Don't know yet."

"Are you always so short with people?"

She was irritating me. "Do you have a low credit score, and why are you asking me so many muthafucking questions?"

Chase's eyes looked as if they were going to tear away from their sockets. "My credit score is none of your business. I'm only trying to make conversation, but I get a feeling that you don't wish to be bothered. Whenever you feel up to a one-on-one, I'm sure you'll be able to find me."

She slightly cut her eyes at me and worked her hips from side to side, as she left the room. She was too sassy, too nosey, too broke, and something in her eyes said trouble. Strike three for her. I preferred to keep my distance.

I stood to stretch and massaged my forehead, trying to relieve the stress. My kids were on my mind, but I honestly needed a break from them as well. I would surely miss them, but it was a wise choice for me to see how everyone back at home would manage without me. With that in mind, I dialed Shane's number, but not before I switched Jada's and Chase's nametags. I hoped to have better luck with Jada.

"I knew you wouldn't be able to do it," Shane said, laughing. "You want me to come pick you up, right?"

"Nope. I want you to bring me my shit. Leave my luggage at the end of the driveway and I'll pick it up from there. I'll get disqualified from the competition if anyone I know is on the premises."

"No problem, but I can't even imagine what it is that you're about to do. I do not believe that you'll make it past one week."

I loved proving Shane wrong. "How much money you got?"

"Plenty."

"Yeah, thanks to me. Therefore, I bet you a quarter of a million dollars that I can and will stay here for the next three months. You down with that bet or not?"

"Three months? With no pussy? Hell, yeah, I'm down with it. More like three days, and best friend or not, I expect for you to pay up."

"Who says I will be without pussy? No matter what, though, my hand will work out just fine. Now, bring me my shit and I'll get at you in three months."

Shane laughed and hung up on me. He gave me the ammunition I needed to go through with this. From this moment on, I was down with whatever swung my way.

I left the bedroom, now looking at the brighter side of this. But as soon as I walked out, Chase was there to greet me.

"Here," she said, giving me a check. "I assume that your attitude stinks because you're out of three-hundred bucks for paying the taxi driver. I hate to do this, but I have a feeling that if I don't give your money back, you're going to make these three months miserable for me."

I took the check from her and looked at it. It was only for two hundred and fifty dollars; she had come up short. Trying to get over was the name of her game, but she had me fucked up. Her address showed that she lived in an area in St. Louis that I was very familiar with. I'll just say the area wasn't anything to brag about.

"I can't accept a check that may bounce in my hand before it reaches the bank. This one has a negative balance, and because of your credibility, I have to reject it."

I ripped the check in several pieces and let the paper fall to the floor. Chase stood with her jaw dropped. "So, that's how you're doing it, huh? I mean, who are you? Where did you come from and how dare you talk to me like that?"

"If you don't like what I have to say, don't confront me with no bullshit again. Just because I paid the taxi driver, it doesn't mean that I took your side. Personally, I think you tried to fuck that man over, but that's just my opinion."

Chase folded her arms across her chest. Much attitude was on display and it was funny to watch her lose control like this. "I would tell you what you can do with your opinion, but you already know, don't you?"

I rubbed my goatee and licked across my lips. "No, I don't know. You seem like a woman who has no problem speaking her mind, so why don't you tell me?"

She threw her hands in the air. "You know what, forget it. I'm not going to waste my time with an arrogant fool like you, and as far as I'm concerned, the taxi incident is a done deal. If you were foolish enough to pay the taxi driver, that was your loss, not mine. I won't try to repay you again, and please don't ask me for your money back."

"I promise I won't. Now, are you done? Is it okay for me to get settled in, now that you got all of that off your chest?"

"If I had any say-so about it, you wouldn't even be allowed to come in here with that attitude. But since I don't, welcome, Mr. Rogers. I hope you somehow manage to knock that chip off your shoulder and have a good time."

"I'm looking forward to it. Hope you are too."

As she choked on her next reply, I stepped around her and walked smoothly toward the door to catch Shane with my luggage. On my way there, I spotted Roc parlaying on the sectional couch with his feet propped on the table. His hands were behind his head and he was watching ESPN. Something about him irked me. Having his feet on the table, as if this were his damn house was tacky.

The overall objective to Hell House was to be the last one standing. I already knew I would be, but I had to skillfully plan this out and get to know how the others operated. Chase had already shown her weakness, so getting her out of here would be easy. It was time to see what was up with Roc.

I made my way down the steps and into the sunken living room. Roc saw me, but pretended as if he didn't. He kept his eyes focused on the TV, but I knew better. That was how I got down, especially when I wanted to make someone think they weren't important. Fucking with him, I reached for one of the magazines underneath his feet on the table.

"Do you mind moving your feet so I can get this?" I said.

Roc continued to look straight ahead. His feet did not move, but his mouth did. "Pull on it."

"Might rip it."

"Your problem, not mine."

"Wrong answer. It's gon' be your problem, if you don't lift your feet off the magazine I want to read."

Roc jumped to his feet and stood several inches away from me. His face was scrunched and madness was upon him. "What's up with you, *nigga?* And who the fuck you talkin' to like that? You need to holla at me like you got some sense. I ain't none of those good-old boys you be hangin' with at the country club, so watch yourself, potnah."

The ghetto made a lot of fools feel as if they were tough and invincible. Obviously, Roc was a product of that environment, but little did he know, so was I. This suit I had on was misleading, and when the time came for me to really get down with this idiot, I would have no problem doing it. For now, I had to accept the country-club membership that he had given me. But before I could say anything, Chase came into the room and stood next to Roc. She looked up at him.

"Chill, all right? He's not worth it, and the last thing I want is for you to get kicked out of here. I'm looking forward to having fun; fun that I thought you were interested in having. Right?"

Roc kept his eyes on me, but he backed up to the couch to sit down. Chase sat next to him, leaving very little breathing room in between them. I smiled to myself, knowing that pushing his buttons would be easy. Ole punk-ass nigga let a manipulative woman take his mind off the ass kicking I was *supposed* to get. That spoke volumes—he was weak.

I snatched the magazine off the table and glanced at the two of them cuddling on the couch. I cleared my throat to get their attention. "Listen. My bad for causing so much confusion, but I must confess that y'all make a real nice couple. Seem to have a lot in common and who knows? Things may work out for the two of you. Good luck with that sista, Roc. Chase seems like a real winner."

I winked and walked away.

"Hey, Jaylin," Chase said, halting my steps. I turned around, only to see her backside. She slapped her hand on her ass, shaking a chunk of it as she gripped it. "Kiss. My. Whole, entire ass, okay?"

For the first time, I smiled. "I would, but I can't get to it because your skirt is in the way."

To no surprise, Chase pulled up her skirt and I'll be damned if she didn't show her pretty ass. It was as pretty and round as I had imagined it to be. And anyone who knew me, they knew I was a man of my word and I loved to be *Naughty*. I walked over to her and bent down. Soaked my lips with my tongue and placed a delicate kiss on her right ass cheek. She blushed when I stood up, but I turned my attention to Roc, who sat on the couch with shock in his eyes.

"Get control of your girl," I said to him. "I think she likes me."

"Man, get on out of here with that shit. And like I said, that sounds like a problem for you, not me. Handle it."

No doubt, I would. I strutted away, but heard Chase say, "Screw you, Jaylin. You're not all that, you know?"

Yes, I was. And by now, she knew it.

Jada

My life had been going downhill since I let my ex-boyfriend, Kiley, get away. But I had to keep it moving. Therefore, when I was contacted about doing this challenge, I was all for it. I needed some excitement in my life. I got tired of sitting around all day arguing with folks on the phone over stupid stuff that didn't even matter. My girlfriends were all haters and all they wanted to do was go to the casino, get wasted at the clubs and eat. I was up to two hundred and thirty pounds now, but no one could deny how cute I was. Not even the man in my life. He wasn't about nothing but selling dope and trying to play hard. He somewhat reminded me of Kiley, but I was a fool if I ever thought I'd find a man to replace him. That man was so good to me and it was funny how I didn't realize all of that until after we had broken up.

My girlfriend, Portia, dropped me off in front of the Hell House, but it didn't look like a Hell House to me. I couldn't wait to get inside to see what was up, so I hurried to remove my bags from the trunk. Portia helped and then she gave me a hug.

"Be safe and write me if you can," she said. "You did say y'all can't have no phones, right?"

"That was one of the stupid rules, but I'mma do my best to keep mine on me. If I can't, then I'll write to let you know what's goin' on."

"You do that, boo, and don't hurt nobody up in there."

"I'll try not to, but you do know your friend."

We laughed.

Portia gave me another hug before she got into the car and drove off. I noticed several pieces of Kenneth Cole luggage at the end of the driveway, and I wondered whom they belonged to. Since I had two heavy bags full of stuff, I made my way up the long driveway and to the front door. By the time I got to it, I was out of breath. My jeans were so tight, they made my muffin top boil over my belt. My Black Girls Rock T-shirt was stretched across my 44 Double D's and the tennis shoes I wore had my toes crammed. It was so hot outside that my sandy-brown Afro was pulled away from my face, allowing the fullness of it to show. I never wore much makeup, only because my entire look was natural and I didn't need it.

I dropped my bags and reached out to knock on the door. What seemed to be seconds later, the door came open. Standing in the door-way was one of the most nice-looking brothers I had ever laid my eyes on. Actually, he was too cute and his cologne was intoxicating. Looked like he could easily be on the down low, and his tan had his body as caramelized as mine. I always made it my business to steer clear of men that I felt looked better than me and he did. His piercing gray eyes scanned me over, then he shot outside without saying one word.

"Excuse you," I said as he bumped my shoulder. "Damn."

I watched as he walked down the driveway to get his luggage. Making sure that he didn't bump me again, I picked up my bags and carried them into the house. It was beautiful inside, and I was in awe, thinking, *How Can I Be Down?* I kept it moving down the hallway and into a living room area where I saw a snooty-looking bitch sitting close to dark-and-damn-sure-lovely. Now, this dude was definitely my type, and my love for 50 Cent had finally come to an abrupt end. I didn't appreciate how close glamour girl was sitting next to him, so I played it cool.

"Hello," I said, sucking in my stomach and pulling down my shirt to make sure that it covered the wideness of my curvy hips. I was happy about my full figure, no doubt, but I wasn't sure if brotha-man appreciated healthy women. Maybe not, since the skinny woman next to him seemed to have his attention. So much so, that when I spoke, he only tossed his head back.

"Hi," the woman next to him said, wiggling her fingers and displaying a fake smile.

"Hello," I replied again, being fake as well. I dropped my bags on the floor and plopped down on the couch. It felt good to take a load off. "So, what's the deal here? Am I late?"

"No," the chick said. "We're still waiting to see what's up." She inched forward and extended her hand. "My name is Chase Jenkins. And you are?"

"I'm Jada Mahoney. It's a pleasant to meet you."

"Pleasure," Chase corrected me. "Not pleasant."

Oh, no, this bitch didn't go there. I realized that I was going to have to chop this heifer up like putting meat in a food processor. She smiled and sat back on the couch. All this fakeness was working me.

I looked up and saw Mr. Hollywood walk by with his luggage, but he didn't say a word to nobody. I wondered what was up with his attitude, but first I had to see what was up with all the dark chocolate sitting next to Chase. He was engrossed in the football game on TV, but I saw him checking me out from the corner of his eye.

"Who playin'?" I asked because I loved to watch football.

Unfortunately, Chase spoke up before he did. "The St. Louis Rams and the Cardinals."

"I was askin' him, though."

He stood and walked toward the kitchen area. "Roc," he said to me. "And she just told you who was playin'."

"Okay, Roc, but what the fuck is up with everybody's attitudes in here? Am I missin' somethin'?"

"Ain't nobody got no attitude, ma," Roc said, opening the refrigerator. He removed two bottled waters and tossed one to me. I caught it. "Just tryin' to check out the game. Handle yo business with yo bags and then come back to the livin' room so we can holla."

Now, he was singing my tune. I was grinning from ear-to-ear and thanked him for the water. Chase told me where I could find the bedroom, so I left to go put my bags in the closet they mentioned. When I opened the door to the bedroom, I couldn't believe my eyes. It was small, but was nice and comfy. I looked for my nametag, noticing that it was right beside Roc's. Chase's was on the other side of his. I figured the fine dude was inside of the walk-in closet because I heard him talking to someone on the phone.

"Because you be bullshitting, baby, that's why," he said to the person over the phone, as I went into the closet. "We'll deal with that when I come home. Until then, stay up and don't be over there crying because you miss me. "

He put his phone in his pocket and then he shot a quick glance at me. I thought he was going to speak, but all he did was turn his back and hang more of his clothes.

The closet was humongous. Other luggage was inside, but no other pieces of clothing were hung. I had my stuff crammed into my bags. I decided to straighten my pieces now, so I didn't have to do it later.

"You almost knocked me down when you rushed outside," I said, looking at the man's backside. Nice, but I was so sure another dude was getting it.

He turned around, scanning his eyes over me once again. His gaze was unnerving in a sense, but I looked at him in the same way.

"If an apology is what you're looking for," he replied nonchalantly. "You're not going to get one, especially since you were in the way."

My brows shot up so fast that my thick eyelashes were about to fall off. Was that his way of calling me fat? I was about to let this arrogant, curly topped-ass fool have it. Men like him made me sick and he needed to take his Harvard degree-carrying tail back to where he came from.

"An apology would be nice, but by the looks of your stuck-up gay ass, I'm sure I won't get it. The next time you bump me, though, expect some piano playin' and dirt layin' to go on. Somebody will be plannin' your funeral 'cause I'm not the one to mess with, just so you know."

He narrowed his eyes and he snickered a little, before turning back around. I wanted to punch him in his face; he was so irritating to me. I understood exactly what his look meant. All it said was I'm better than you and you ain't shit. Some black people killed me with that mess. Act like they ain't been through nothing and always looking down on other folks. By the time this Hell House mess was over with, he was going to learn to respect me. I would make sure of that.

I moved over to the side of the closet where he was to hang my things. His name-brand clothes were neatly hung and a few shirts were folded on top of the racks. I thought about what he did for a living.

Probably sold drugs or had somebody selling for him. I wanted to ask, but a smart response could get spit in his face.

"You're either Prince or Jaylin," I assumed. "Probably Prince, since you're up in here actin' like the Almighty One."

"I'm whoever you want me to be. Gay, dead, a prince...take your pick."

"Ugh. How about an asshole then? Can you be one of those, especially since you're actin' like one?"

"I can do that, but first I may have to shove my dick in your mouth to silence that nonsense you're talking. Then, if I start calling you names that you're not going to like, your feelings gon' get hurt. Several words are on the tip of my tongue, so back the fuck up."

I tightened my fist, knowing that this fool was about to get it if he dissed me. Some men needed to be put in their place, and if I could handle Kiley, I definitely could handle him.

"Say it," I threatened, inching closer to him with gritted teeth. "I dare you."

The evil-looking bastard didn't appreciate my words or that I had moved closer to him. If I swung on him, there wasn't much room in the closet for me to get him good how I wanted to. So for now, I was thinking about scratching his face and poking those gray, disturbing eyes out with my fingers. He could tell that I was plotting to do something, so he backed up and shot me another stern gaze that was supposed to scare me.

"I don't know you, and I certainly don't know what the hell your problem is," he said. "But let me say this...you have crossed over into territory that you don't want to be in. If you want to keep getting at me like some kind of gangbanger, I will feel threatened. And if I feel threatened, that means, woman or not, you will find yourself knocked out cold on the fucking floor behind you. From this moment on, you need to think carefully about how you get at me."

He turned around and started straightening his things again. In no way did I view this fool as a man who would put his hands on a woman or hurt her. He looked too soft and his appearance showed that he was some kind of uppity nerd that would probably run home to tell his mama about me hurting his feelings. I was so annoyed by his sharp tone, by the way he kept looking at me, and because he had bumped my shoulder and still hadn't apologized for it. Not to mention that he had just threatened me. That was why I couldn't let this fool get away with what he'd done.

I tapped his shoulder to confront him again, and he swung around with madness visible in his eyes. Without any warning, he reached out his hand and gripped it around my neck. After that, several things happened and my entire body shut down. My breathing halted and my blood felt as if it had stopped flowing. I could not move, and I could barely see from the tears in my eyes clouding my vision. When I tried to turn my neck, he strengthened his grip and that was it for me. I felt hypnotized, and I was now in his command.

"Now that I have your attention," he said with a slow nod. "And I do have your attention, don't I?"

I followed suit and slowly nodded because he had added even more pressure to my neck when he squeezed tighter.

"Good. But now that I do have it, I want you to listen up and keep your big mouth shut. Can you do that for me?"

More pressure, so I slowly nodded again.

"I love progress, even when it has to be forced upon those who don't always know better. You do know better, don't you?"

I nodded again and all he did was smirk.

"I thought so, but in case you don't, I want to share a few things with you, just so we don't get off on the wrong foot while we're here. My name is Jaylin Rogers and you shall not refer to me as anything else. I'm a straight man, and I do not take bullshit from others too lightly. I will make yo ass pay for fucking with me, and if you feel as though you can't control yourself when you're around me, then I suggest that you keep distance between us. Because the next time you interrupt me with your bullshit, the punishment will be nothing like this. What I will do to you will hurt, and the last thing I want to do is go around hurting women. Maybe with my dick, but surely not with my hands."

At that moment, he snatched his hand back and it seemed that my whole body started functioning again. I could breathe, I could move my mouth and my blood was pumping. Iron Man turned back around, ignoring me again. I opened my mouth wide to suck in air I had lost, and I rubbed my neck, making sure it was still there. I didn't know if I had been unconscious or not, and it felt like he had done some type of voodoo shit on me. That was so messed up, but I had to let him know that his actions weren't cool. This time, I didn't tap his shoulder and I preferred to keep my distance.

"Uh, excuse me, but what in the hell did you just do to me? Please don't ever put your hands on me again, and if you think that a choke-hold is going to silence me, you are sadly mistaken."

"I swear, some muthafucking hoes prefer to learn things the hard way," he said, shaking his head, but not turning around. When I looked up and saw another chick waiting to put her things in the closet, I stormed out of it. I was further away from him, so I felt safe talking back and responding to his hoe comment.

"Stupid bastard, the name is Jada!" I shouted from outside of the closet, per his request to keep distance between us. "Oooo, just wait! I got somethin' for that ass! You gon' be somewhere leakin', trust me!"

I marched out of the bedroom, thinking of ways to get him back for what he'd done to me. I also wasn't sure if coming to this house was the right doggone decision, and the last thing I wanted to do was fistfight with men. That was something I'd done mostly all my life, and I was sick of it. Maybe my approach toward that idiot was wrong. I did want to start off on the right foot, but after what he'd done, I didn't know if that was possible.